John Paul Carinci is president of Carinci Insurance Agency, Inc., an author, songwriter, poet, and CEO of Better Off Dead Productions, Inc., a movie production company. As a worldwide published author, John's books include: *An All-Consuming Desire To Succeed*, *The Power of Being Different*, *In Exchange of Life*, *Share Your Mission #5*, *A Second Chance*, *The Psychic Boy Detective*, *Better Off Dead*, *Better Off Dead In Paradise*, *Defying Death In Hagerstown*, *Awesome Success Principles and Quotations*, *The Two Lives Of Everett Quinn*, *There's An Angel Inside Of Me, An Angel In Training,* and *The Quest For Purpose.*

For my wife, Vera.
For all those who inspire authors to continue to create with newfound imagination.

John Paul Carinci

A PSYCHIC CRIME SOLVER

AUSTIN MACAULEY PUBLISHERS™
LONDON • CAMBRIDGE • NEW YORK • SHARJAH

Copyright © John Paul Carinci 2021

All rights reserved. No part of this publication may be reproduced, distributed, or transmitted in any form or by any means, including photocopying, recording, or other electronic or mechanical methods, without the prior written permission of the publisher, except in the case of brief quotations embodied in critical reviews and certain other non-commercial uses permitted by copyright law. For permission requests, write to the publisher.

Any person who commits any unauthorized act in relation to this publication may be liable to criminal prosecution and civil claims for damages.

This is a work of fiction. Names, characters, businesses, places, events, locales, and incidents are either the products of the author's imagination or used in a fictitious manner. Any resemblance to actual persons, living or dead, or actual events is purely coincidental.

Ordering Information
Quantity sales: Special discounts are available on quantity purchases by corporations, associations, and others. For details, contact the publisher at the address below.

Publisher's Cataloging-in-Publication data
Carinci, John Paul
A Psychic Crime Solver

ISBN 9781647500887 (Paperback)
ISBN 9781647500894 (ePub e-book)

Library of Congress Control Number: 2021921671

www.austinmacauley.com/us

First Published 2021
Austin Macauley Publishers LLC
40 Wall Street, 33rd Floor, Suite 3302
New York, NY 10005
USA

mail-usa@austinmacauley.com
+1 (646) 5125767

Chapter One

She was a young woman, desperately running all out. A man was chasing her, and she was losing ground. I heard her frantically screaming at no one around. The moonlit night revealed her clearly. There was a blood-curdling scream as he grabbed her from behind, spun her around, and down onto the ground. Then a higher-pitched scream.

It was a powerful downward thrust as I saw the large knife go deep into the woman's chest.

She quickly folded into nothingness as I clearly heard her last loud, defeated moan.

She was on the ground motionless as the tall, muscular man hovered over her like a victorious tiger inspecting his latest prey. He stood motionless, studying his slaughter, staring closer now for any residual movement. In the still of the night, there was no movement. How could there be? The life quickly left the young woman of perhaps twenty. A blonde, slim, tall young woman was now dead.

Why was I shown this image? Why am I allowed to see so many images that others never witness? I knew I had psychic abilities ever since the early age of 12. They started out suddenly.

The visions are sometimes quick, sometimes long, sometimes heart-wrenching, sometimes impossible to stomach. This was just such a vision. Why me? Why now? Why so graphic and intense? I've asked these questions of God so very many times. I've surrendered, trying to stop all visions of any kind. I have begged so many times that the visions cease forever, but to no avail. I was assured on so many occasions from the hereafter that this was my calling. That we each have a calling, and I had been carefully chosen to fulfill a huge void in society. I communicate regularly with a spirit guide that convinces me I was called to this service.

Still, at times I feel as if I can go no further. I want it all to end, no matter what consequence it may have on society or anyone else. Then something happens, and I feel the intense satisfaction inside from truly changing one person's life forever. The intense highs outweigh the lowest lows of depression I feel at times. It is a trying life, this psychic life.

It happens so often, this tremendous inner peace of helping ease the pain of someone so traumatized with grief that that alone is enough for me to accept just one more day, just one more vision, just one last time. That never seems to end. My spirit reminds me often: "Welcome to the life of a psychic."

It also is my spirit guide that reinforces my need to continue. Why brutal visions, I ask. Why so much pain and suffering so often? I don't receive accurate answers to those questions, only the realization that life plays out in cycles. There is good. There is evil. There is love. There is hatred. There are happy times. There are tremendously painful times of loss. It all runs in cycles. No one is exempt from pain and suffering and loss, sometimes in the cycles of their own lives.

I have been hand-selected, I have been assured, to ease the ultimate life-long despair many suffer after such losses and murder and deaths of infants.

I have been hearing voices and seeing visions of people for most of my seventy years on Earth. As a child, it started quite innocently at first. I believed my stuffed animals and play dolls had voices. I thought they were all alive. I thought they were speaking to me as my own personal friends. I felt quite fortunate, as my best friends all informed me that their toys never spoke to them.

When they would come to my home, they all waited patiently for voices to come out of my toys, but there were no voices, no visions, no thoughts or communication of any kind, not even for me when friends were with me.

Everyone thought I was lying, that I was making it all up for attention. My parents just humored me during my younger days. They believed that I just had a great imagination. My parents kept telling friends and relatives that I would grow up to be a famous author of fantasy novels.

I believed everyone. I knew that I heard voices, saw visions, and had friends who were in far-off places that no one else could see or hear. But it was my own world. It was special to me, even though I couldn't understand it all.

The voices at first were quite friendly, with no real motives except to comfort me, be my friends from afar. They were the voices of children and infants who had passed away at young ages. Their only motive, I realized, was to play with me while I played with my own toys. Secret friends, I couldn't talk about to anyone.

At times, they would show me their own toys and dolls, though some looked to be very old, like antiques. Little did I know at that time some of the children had been deceased for many decades or centuries.

They each would tell me their names and would return pretty frequently. Some would introduce me to new friends that I could visualize with the regular friend. Never did any of the early visions try to frighten me or tell me about their deaths. I just believed that these spirit friends chose me over anyone else because I had unique toys, not because I was that much different.

It took years before any spirits showed me death and devastation of any kind. I remember when I visualized the first death of a spirit friend. I didn't want to see it, but the spirit, Holly, asked me to remain calm as she tried to show me how she passed on and into the hereafter.

I knew she wasn't sharing Earth with me. I finally derived that after the first few years of visits from Holly. But I never focused on any of the spirits' deaths. It just never was important. We would just play and talk.

I must have been twelve when Holly, one day, took it upon herself to show me how she died. I was devastated at first, unable to see my friend of so many years die. She told me, "You know, I am not alive on your Earth?"

"Yes, Holly, I realized that you are visiting me from Heaven."

"That is correct, Marjorie. I passed away at a young age. But don't be scared or feel sorry for me. You see, we all live on in a very special life in Heaven. Although so many people cry and feel very sad when someone so young should pass away, they should actually feel happy that the person passed on from their Earth to the world of the hereafter."

"But we don't want you to die and go to the afterlife. It hurts us so much."

"Yes, we know that we leave so many behind in such pain. But they should be happy we go on forever in the hereafter. You see, Marjorie, everyone passes away from your world and graduates to the afterlife!"

"Graduates? Holly, I don't understand."

"Just as children graduate each year from school, Marjorie, all earthlings must one day pass on. This is a most pleasant passing and should be celebrated as such."

"Why should we celebrate losing our loved one?"

"Because they enter into an eternity filled with unconditional love, the reuniting with all those who passed before them, and unlimited learning and knowledge they could never receive on Earth."

"So those who graduate first are basically rewarded."

"Oh, yes. They are rewarded greatly for living a life on Earth that is very challenging and difficult."

"I see. But we still are going to be sad no matter how much we understand this."

"Yes, we know this, and that is okay. You no longer see that loved one on Earth anymore. But they see you. They sense every joy and pain you will ever feel. You are surrounded every day by their love. This you can be sure of."

"I do feel better about that."

"Yes. Feel free to communicate with them as you do with me, even though you can't see them. They are there. They are with you now, surrounding you with love."

"I love you, Grandma."

"Yes, she knows this well. Marjorie, I want you to see how I passed from your world many years ago. But please do not be sad for me. Be happy because I am so happy in Heaven, Okay?

"It was over a hundred years ago in Earth time. I was swimming with my cousins in the ocean in my country of Russia. I went out to the deep section of the ocean as my cousins stayed in shallow waters. As I was a good swimmer at the age of 12, I was suddenly drawn out to the deeper waters. I tried to fight the current, drawing me farther out, but I was losing the battle.

"I felt the water go past my neck and rise to my chin and mouth. I struggled, but my feet wouldn't work in getting me back to shore. So, I went under, trying to swim back to the shore. But the strong current only pulled me into deeper waters.

"I knew I would die as I held my breath and tried to save all of my oxygen. But as I was accepting the fact that I would be dying, suddenly an angel, under the water, hugged me. He was smiling and shaking his head, *yes*, reassuring me that death would be fine.

"As he embraced me, the pain from the lack of oxygen and crying subsided. In a split second, I was transported to another place. I was suddenly enveloped in bright light and felt a great sense of love and kindness. I was in Heaven. So, be happy for me, Marjorie. Do not feel bad that my life on

Earth ended because life never ends. It continues for eternity."

"So, you went directly to Heaven?"

"We all go to Heaven, Marjorie. It is like nothing you could ever imagine in your head. It is *Paradise*."

"So, Holly, what about hell?"

"There is no hell. That is something entirely invented by people on Earth over all the years. It doesn't exist."

"But we were taught that people who do bad things go straight to hell and suffer."

"Yes, but it doesn't exist. We will talk much more about this and many other things at a later time. Marjorie, I will be with you for your entire life on Earth.

"When you were born, you were chosen to help others in an extraordinary way. I was assigned to you, and you only knew me as your special secret friend that no one else could see or hear. Well, actually, I am what is known as a *Spirit Guide*."

Chapter Two

It was two months later, after the young woman I witnessed in a vision was savagely murdered. I was being interviewed live on WFLA-AM Radio in Fort Lauderdale, Florida, where I live.

"Welcome back, listeners. We have a very special guest with us on the Judy Crimmens show this afternoon. It is a real treat to welcome my unique guest, Marjorie Chapman, a self-proclaimed Medium, a Psychic.

"I understand you were born in England, Marjorie, and moved here many years ago?"

"Yes, Judy, that is true. Thanks for having me on your show. It is so good to be here. I listen to your radio station every day."

"Well, we are very excited to have you here. You are the very first psychic medium we ever had on the show. And I must admit I never met a psychic before. So, before we begin, why don't you enlighten us and tell us a little about yourself, if you will."

"Well, I have lived in Fort Lauderdale for nearly forty years now. I was born in England and was raised there, as well as received my education there. I must say, though, I love the Florida weather here so much better!"

"Yes, it is easier on one's bones. So, tell us how you first realized you had psychic abilities? I imagine it was quite a shock of sorts, suddenly seeing and hearing things others don't see or hear?"

"No, Judy, it was quite the opposite, in fact. You see, very early on, as a little girl, I saw and heard other children. They were my secret friends. It was not strange at all. I just assumed that these child spirits were my personal friends, that they liked to be only with me, which is why others couldn't see or hear them.

"I was never frightened by seeing the spirits, mostly because I was so young. The spirits at that time never showed anything but fun and playthings to me."

"I see," Judy said with a nervous smile. "I don't think I could do what you do, Marjorie. I would be too scared. I would probably faint outright."

"Oh, it really isn't that scary, Judy. The spirits in the afterlife mean no harm to us at all. They, some of them, are not settled into their new life yet. While some others are very disturbed about past events that happened on Earth during their existence here. Some just have to vent. Some want to right a terrible wrong that was done to them or someone else. While others still need desperately to reach out to their very distraught loved ones that are in so much pain from their passing."

"So, they reach out to you, who in turn can reach their loved ones on Earth and ease their concerns?"

"Yes, exactly. We, the really talented psychics, can zero in on the intended loved ones that our spirit friends need to reach and satisfy that they are fine and content in the afterlife. The message is fairly consistent in that there is existence after death, and we all will be together again."

"That, honestly, is so hard to accept for many people. I know that I am one, Marjorie. I would freak out if a spirit spoke to me."

"I bet you would be fine. But knowing that you wouldn't be too receptive in receiving messages, the spirits would communicate to you through others like myself."

"So, Marjorie, when did you realize that you had a special gift and it wasn't just an overactive imagination?"

"It was some years after when the spirits would tell me things that only a few people alive would understand. That was when I knew I had a special gift and that I could actually use my gift to help others."

"Was there ever a time that you wished you didn't have this ability? That you were sorry, you could see and hear things many others can't?"

"Oh, yes, Judy. I'm afraid that there were a few times when I silently prayed to the spirits in the afterlife to stop all messages. That I just couldn't handle it any longer."

"And why was that? Why would you risk shutting off such an amazing gift?"

"At first, playing with my spirit friends at such an early age was an absolute blast. They were like the best friends anyone could ever want. They were like sisters, always there for me. But slowly, as I got much older, I was communicating with spirits that needed me to see their own troubled pasts while they were alive.

"I would see many deaths, murders, brutal acts, and much despair. It was almost too much to bear. My original spirit guide, Holly, who came to me when I was very young, still appeared to me. She will be with me forever, she told me. But with her help, I am able to communicate with other spirits that are still in despair or need to communicate with their loved ones still alive.

"So, Judy, when I see how a spirit was brutally murdered while on Earth or died tragically in a car wreck, I sometimes want to just end this psychic gift I have and return to normalcy of some sort."

"So, you actually do see how and when someone was brutally murdered, gore and all?"

"Yes, the spirits tell me that I need to see why they are still not at peace. Whether it is because their murderers were never brought to justice or there is still some secret out there that only the spirits themselves can clear up."

"So, Marjorie, that brings me to the latest news on your solving a murder and helping the authorities with your unique psychic abilities. I understand from the media that a woman who was murdered recently contacted you from the hereafter. Can you share that story with us, please?"

"Sure. We know that there are spirits that are desperate to reach out to someone and vent. They need to right a wrong or reach loved ones who are so distraught that the surviving loved ones here stop living their lives. The troubled survivors grieve so much they forget or lose their desire to live their own lives, caught up in despair over their deceased loved ones.

"So, through my spirit guide, Holly, who I've known forever, the spirit of Agnes Schnitter, age 22, came to me. She showed me a complete scene of how she was savagely murdered. It appeared to me, as happens quite often, late at night.

"Sometimes a vision will hit you like a ton of bricks, hard and fast, and quite painful. This was one of those visions, one of those times I pleaded with my spirit guide to let it end. That, of course, never works. When a vision is meant to be viewed by a spirit, nothing will get in its way.

"So, I saw a young barefoot woman running from a park with a large man chasing after her. She was screaming and pleading for her life, to no avail. The high-pitch scream confirmed what I saw as the knife penetrated deep into her chest.

"I watched helplessly as the life drained out of her. I understand that death on Earth is never the end but rather a new story in a new location, but it never stops hurting to see what spirits show me of their passing, be it a tragic killing, accident, or natural passing. It still hurts to visualize the survivors' pain, grief, and despair.

"So, Agnes Schnitter showed me how she died on a lonely, dark, cold street in Rocky Mount, North Carolina. She had died over a year before, but the case was cold, with no leads for the authorities to follow up on. Agnes sought my help to allow the authorities to solve the murder. She wanted the killer to rot behind bars for life, so he couldn't repeat the act on other women.

"She was beautiful with long blonde hair, a cute nose, and hazel eyes. As she communicated with me, she showed me that she was slim and tall, like a model. She showed me the Starbucks store where she had been a barista for a year and a half. Agnes explained that is where the killer was attracted to her. He was a customer of the coffee shop, but she didn't know him and never had words with him.

"Agnes told me she was returning from a night out with her girlfriend at a bar. She was cutting through the park as a shortcut to get home when she encountered the large man.

"She knew nothing about the man except that he must have been stalking her. He attacked her in the park, ripping her clothes and sexually attacking her. She fought, kicking and clawing, but he was forcing her down and bloodied her face. Only when they fought near a park bench. She said she kicked him hard with a knee to the stomach and broke free. Agnes said she ran for her life until he caught her and killed her.

"She did describe the man, and I saw what he looked like too: tall, big-boned, about six-foot-two, and maybe two-seventy. He appeared to her to be around forty-five, with no rings, no facial hair, and a receding hairline of black hair, no doubt dyed.

"Then we finally had something to help the authorities. It was when they were fighting in the park that Agnes remembered something very valuable. The man, with her blood on his hands from her face, grabbed under the park bench. There would be a good chance that the blood he and she had drawn, which was on his hands, would be under the park bench and may contain his fingerprints."

"How amazing that was," Judy said. "Only this deceased woman would know this, Marjorie. Were you shocked at the message she shared with you?"

"I was flabbergasted that a spirit could send not only a full vision that plays out like a high-definition movie, but she had so much more in details that she communicated to me."

"So, how exactly does the communication process work? Do you hear voices? Do the spirits ever touch you? I would faint dead on the floor! I'm telling you, I get chills just thinking about it all."

"No, it's not really voices. It's more like thoughts so strong that you know for sure it is not an overactive imagination."

"So, the woman thinks of you, and you know…"

"I sense thoughts and see a visual of the woman, much like a movie playing out. The spirit thinks, and I sense and see it all. They think about a house, and I see it. I see the color of the bricks, the roof color, the landscaping, everything. It is amazing, really. I could be in a coffee shop and eating a bagel and having tea. Suddenly, a new spirit will appear in my mind. I will see them, know all about them quickly and why they feel the urgent need to break into my quiet, personal time."

"Amazing. They just come to you like that?"

"Yes. It could be for the purpose of communicating to one of the patrons in the store, or there is an immediate need to reach out to someone present that I have never met before."

"So, what do you do?"

"What I do is put my bagel down, get up, and approach the person the spirit has chosen to communicate with. I go over to the person, say, 'Excuse me, I am Marjorie, and I need to speak with you for a few minutes if I may.' Then, for example, I tell them that their Uncle Joe wishes to speak with them by speaking through me, that I am a psychic, and their uncle came to me out of nowhere while I was eating a bagel. 'Does the black bible mean anything to you?' Like I told one person once.

"The person says, 'Wow, my uncle gave me that black bible for my Confirmation when I was very young.' It goes down something like that."

"Fantastic, really! Marjorie, you sure have an amazing gift. Does it ever simmer down? In other words, does spirit ever give you a break and allow you just to live your life, or are they always vying for position in your mind, so to speak?"

"Great question. It is incredible, really. Sometimes I will have total peace and quiet, but at other times there are so many spirits that try to push their way into the front of my mind. It could be because the deceased mother of someone is telling me a story to relay to their surviving daughter. Still, the grandmother of the survivor wants the story to be relayed according to her recollection. Which is a different version. There could sometimes be five spirits waiting in the wings. It can get very hectic at times.

"But when I am completely exhausted and can no longer tolerate more spirit interaction, I just tell my spirit guide, Holly, who is always silently there in the background, that I need quiet time. She then turns the noise and vision all off for me."

"Can we go back to the young woman, Agnes Schnitter, as I see in my notes here? Whatever happened to the investigation there?"

"Well, as expected, the killer did have an extensive criminal history of rape and assault. But he never was convicted for murder. The fingerprints from the underside of the park bench were his downfall, though he was free for over a year till the authorities, with Agnes' help through me, were able to give the evidence needed.

"The killer, Gary Abliss, age 43, was tried and convicted for murder. He will spend the rest of his life in prison."

"How does that make you feel, Marjorie?"

"I feel both ecstatic and very sad at the same time. I am ecstatic about helping Agnes right a wrong. I feel so pleased with helping the family get a little extra closure with their daughter's death, which they have thanked me so much for. But I am sad about the life of the killer, Gary Abliss. That may sound very strange to many people listening, Judy, but I see a waste of human life not only in the life of Agnes but also in the rest of Gary's life.

"What kind of life did that man have? It's almost as if he was put on Earth for no reason at all. He will wither away in prison, just left with the memories of the brutal acts he performed in his past. What purpose was his life about? Perhaps he should never have been born, is what I am battling about inside. But in answer to your question, this is what I deal with in so many cases I am faced with."

"Extraordinary insight, Marjorie. Thank you for sharing your stories on our show. Our listeners and I appreciate you and what you do so much."

"Judy, I have some insight into your life if you would like me to share it now?"

"Uh oh. I was a little worried about this…"

"Not to worry. It's all good once we realize that spiritual life is nothing more to each of us than our loved ones who pass before us needing to remain constant in our lives. They watch over and silently root us on in our own earthly journey. They realize all the emotions we battle with on a daily basis, and they try to assure us in any way they can that it all will be all right and we will all be reunited in the future."

"Marjorie, I so often think of the ones who have died. I wondered if they were ever up above looking down on me. We may say that we believe in life after death, in God, in Heaven, and that good will always prevail over evil. But many of us, though we may not admit it, have great doubts about a great many things."

"Well, I am here to set the record straight. There is a hereafter, a Heaven, spirit life, and they do watch over us and are very aware of everything we do."

"I want to believe. I really do."

"Well, they are in this room all around us now, your loved ones. You may be able to see the orb lights."

"I didn't want to say anything before, but I did see moving white balls of light. I just thought that was my imagination, you know. Then you start to imagine all kinds of things."

"Well, I have an older woman with perfectly styled hair telling me over and over the name, Tusie. She says, 'Tell her Tusie!'"

"Oh my God. That is my grandmother. We always called her Tusie. Her formal name was Cortusa. I can't believe it!"

"She said you always would jump up and down on her lap, very active, always out of control, and she would yell, 'Calm now, baby, calm now!'"

"Yes, she did. I would think her lap was the back of a horse, and I wanted to ride her. I was so bad!"

"Cortusa wants you to know that she is fine and is with all her cousins and sister, Ella. And Dad, Dad, as you called him, is with her smiling down on you right now. They want you to know that we all will be together again. Not to fear anything."

"Oh, yes, Dad, Dad. We always played Hide-and-Seek, and he made believe he never could find me until I came out of hiding, laughing. He made me feel like a queen. He was the best grandfather anyone could ever have."

Chapter Three

Our radio interview went very well. So many people contacted me and commented on my psychic business, wanting to book a reading with me. The next day that I was to meet my best friend, Valerie Taragie, for dinner at Luigi's Italian, the best Italian restaurant in town.

I met Valerie some twenty years earlier, when we both were employed at Doctor Rutter's Veterinarian Service. She was the assistant to the doctor, and I was the office manager. We hit it off right away and have been best friends ever since.

Valerie lost her husband several years ago, and I lost mine in a terrible car wreck some eleven years back. We were married over twenty years ago. My first marriage in England to Alvin Slinnins ended after five years because of abuse from my husband, as he was an alcoholic with a terrible temper. Alcohol has different effects on different people. Alvin got real nasty after only two drinks. Alvin would get jealous for no reason at all and hit me. After five years, I divorced him, leaving him and England behind me. I couldn't stomach the man any longer.

I stayed single after that and relocated at age 30 to Lauderdale-by-the-Sea. The warmth, the humid air, and the nice, friendly people helped me forget my past. I stayed single, afraid of men till I met the accountant love of my life. I was age forty. It was the start of my new life, a life that had slowly passed me by!

We had 19 years of the most wonderful times imaginable. We vacationed to faraway and exotic places: Hawaii, Spain, Greece, and Ireland. I never was able to have children with either marriage. It was difficult at first, but as time went on, it was acceptable. After all, it was a blessing not having children with an alcoholic; and after age 40, it would have been very hard, especially since my second marriage was brand new at age 40.

It was Rodney's second marriage, too. His wife died of ovarian cancer at age 36. They couldn't have children either. His accounting practice was lucrative, and we were comfortable. Rodney was so supportive of my psychic ability and the many readings I would do, primarily for friends and relatives. I charged very little then. But since Rodney's death, I had to charge more for each reading. Valerie now books all my appointments and keeps my schedule for me.

We were in Luigi's Italian Restaurant having a glass of chardonnay. Valerie was quite excited as we spoke about my radio interview. "Marjorie, you were awesome on that show. The telly has been ringing off the wall. We now have booked for months. So many people…"

"Valerie, I didn't know you had a telly like my telly."

"I know you so long now that your accent and vocabulary is contagious," she laughed.

"I know. I have that effect on people."

"Well, you blew everyone away, including Judy, the host, when you brought in her family."

"You know me long enough to know that I don't control the visions, the voices, or the spirits that need me to convey their messages. They are there whenever they have the need to be there. The spirits of the moment are here right now, Valerie. Sometimes they will get the message and go on their way. But when they are desperately intense, trying to get through to someone who is present, well, there is little I can do to shut them down."

"I can tell at times, like now, Marjorie. I can see many orbs all around you. Thank God all the people here in the restaurant can't tell about the orbs or the spirits because there could be a stampede trying to escape the restaurant."

"That being said, Valerie, you know what I have to do, don't you?"

"Of course. You go for it, girl. You go for it! I'll be right here if you need anything, okay?"

"Thanks for understanding, friend!"

I was fortunate that the selected people in the restaurant were seated toward the corner of the left side. I looked carefully at the couple sitting at the table before I dared approach their table.

Slowly, I walked closer, smiling as I looked at the couple. I learned years earlier that you need to approach slowly and speak softly. You must allow the person to acknowledge who you are and precisely what you are trying to tell them. People, in general, are very suspicious, as they should be, of someone snookering them. So, until they accept the fact that I am for real and not looking for anything from them, then and only then will they be receptive to any message I would convey to them.

I always approach the female first. Female to female, smiling, eyes sparkling and calm. She looked sweet to me. She had a loving look about her. I only imagined her pain at the loss of her young daughter. To lose a child is the worst eternal pain a parent could ever be subjected to.

Her name was Karen, and she was a blonde, big-boned woman, just as spirit showed me in my vision earlier. Her daughter told me that it was three years earlier that she passed. The parents were devastated, seeking professional counseling for years.

"Hi, Karen. I'm Marjorie, Marjorie Chapman. Can I sit for a minute?"

She looked puzzled. "Do I know you?" she said as she took the hand I had reached out to shake hers with. Her husband just stared at me and smiled.

"Karen and Jerry, I am a psychic, and I know about you both. I have communicated with spirit, and they asked me to give you a message. Can I sit and share their message with you?"

Their mouths were slightly open in shock as Karen's eyes welled up. They both rose and pulled out a chair for me to sit down at. "My God, please, won't you join us, Marjorie? Please excuse us for being suspects, but we see so many things these days," Karen said.

"Yes, welcome, Marjorie," Jerry added.

"Please, Karen and Jerry, do not feel bad. I get this all the time. Quite honestly, it takes some time before most people take me seriously. That being said, I was at the table over there with my good friend. But, suddenly, I was overcome by a message from spirit. It was your daughter's spirit…"

"Oh, my God. I can't believe it. I think of her every minute of the day. We miss her so much!"

"Yes, and that is what Cynthia disclosed to me. Karen and Jerry, it is important to Cynthia that you are assured that she is fine and content in the afterlife. She requested that I relay this message to you. Sometimes spirit has urgent messages that need to be conveyed to the surviving loved ones, and they just force their way into my mind, even while dining."

"Oh, please, forgive us, Marjorie. Please invite your guest to join us. Don't leave her by herself," Karen said through her tears.

Valerie hurried over to sit with us after I motioned to her. We all made our introductions and continued.

"Now, Karen and Jerry, this is not a formal session, which we may want to do some time in the future; but as I said in the beginning, Cynthia wants you to rest assured that she is here with us right now, that she watches over you both every day. But most importantly, Cynthia wants you to go on living your lives.

"She tells me you don't go out much anymore, and the only reason you are here tonight is that it is your anniversary."

"Oh, my God. How can you know all these things?"

"I don't even know why exactly. But I have been chosen by many spirits to give messages to their loved ones for them. It has been many years now. And quite honestly, it is simply marvelous at times, like now. Happy Anniversary. How many blessed years is it now?"

"It has been 33 years, thank you."

"Wonderful," I said, as Valerie looked on in amazement. She usually does this whenever present for an impromptu reading like this.

"Marjorie, please, what can you tell us about our beautiful Cynthia?" Karen asked.

"Karen, Cynthia says your nickname for her was Pipi because she was very tiny."

"Oh, yes. Cynthia was petite," Karen said as the tears ran.

"Her passing was a little over three years ago?"

"Yes," Jerry said. "It was tragic."

"Cynthia has shared that with me. She was an only child. She passed at 19 and was attending Fort Lauderdale College. She was supposed to attend a concert the night she died…"

"Yes, yes, a Taylor Swift concert. Cynthia was supposed to go with her friends to the concert," Karen said.

"Yes," Jerry added. "She and her three girlfriends were supposed to go, but Cynthia never made it to the concert. She ended up dead on the beach, some ten miles away. Her girlfriends thought she just changed her mind at the last second and didn't want to go to the concert. These things happen with teens, so no one thought anything of it. Not until she was discovered dead."

"It was thought that Cynthia might have overdosed on drugs, self-administered, of course, due to pain?"

"Yes," Karen said. "She had torn ligaments in her ankle from a sports injury while playing a game of soccer. She had been taking Celebrex, but was still in much pain. So, when there were drugs found in her system after death, we believed she tried extra drugs because of the severe pain she was in."

"Yes," I agreed. "But Cynthia wants you to know that it didn't happen that way at all. She desperately needs to set the record straight, but more importantly to assure you both that she, in fact, did not take her life that night."

Karen and Jerry agreed we would take a break and eat our meals, and continue later that evening at their home. Of course, they insisted on us remaining at their table as their guests and paid for Valerie's and my dinners.

We became good friends as the evening unfolded. They wanted to know all about me and, as everyone wanted, to know about my special gift, how long I had been doing it, and the unique spirits I had communicated with. They also wanted to know about any celebrities I had been visited by. And if there were any scandals I had uncovered.

"I really can't talk about individual cases where the authorities were involved, as they are confidential. But there were celebrities who were determined to set the record straight, just as Cynthia was so determined to get a message through to you both tonight.

"There were famous people; one wanted their family to know that their death from a car accident was the fault of a hit-and-run driver who never was brought to justice. Another very famous actress disclosed that she was drowned by a man rather than fell overboard on a boat at sea. That person is currently being investigated by the FBI due to my disclosure to them.

"In Cynthia's case, as is common in the spirit world, they have a special knack for convincing others to do as they wish. In other words, Cynthia, knowing you both would be celebrating an anniversary at the famous Italian restaurant you both love, put the thought of going there tonight myself. It worked. The idea came over me this afternoon, quite suddenly, and I suggested it to Valerie. The rest is history.

"Now, I will be calling the authorities in the morning, just so you are both aware. There was definitely foul play involved in Cynthia's death…"

"Oh, my God! I knew something was missing," Karen shouted, then completely fell apart, crying uncontrollably. Jerry had tears in his eyes as well as Valerie, who hates to show emotions to people she has just met. I felt both bad and glad at the same time. I was glad that Cynthia finally was able to share the truth after more than three years since her murderer pulled the wool over everyone's eyes.

I explained to her parents that I could not disclose all the details of the passing of Cynthia. And I needed to wait until the FBI opened up. And that documents and evidence I will provide to the best of my communication with Cynthia.

"My contact, Carl Higgins, of the FBI, who is an agent I have worked closely with on a few cases, will contact you with much more information. Please be patient."

"We have been nothing but patient for over three years," Jerry said. "We knew all along there was more to the story of our beautiful daughter's death. A few more days won't kill us…"

"Can you tell us just a little more?" Karen begged.

"I will tell you this," I said as I walked closer to hug both of who were seated on the couch. "I can disclose that Cynthia was killed by someone she knew well. Someone who made sexual advances on her. She tried to turn him away before the drugs he forced on her took effect."

"Was she sexually violated?" Jerry asked as his red eyes teared.

"I can't go too far here, but Cynthia disclosed that the man ultimately backed off when he thought his identity was in jeopardy. Cynthia, of course, could not run with her ankle injury. The last piece I can share is the man was older and not a student. But it was most definitely someone Cynthia knew well."

It was after one a.m. when Valerie and I said our good nights to Karen and Jerry Green. I believed that a tremendous weight had been lifted from their shoulders as I assured them that justice would prevail in the capture of Cynthia's murderer. I would stay in touch with them.

Chapter Four

It happens suddenly—first, the inability to move a muscle. The screaming for the vision to stop, to no avail. Fully knowing that it is a dream, but no less terrifyingly painful and torturous. I can sense myself screaming to no one. There is no sound coming from the silent but desperate pleas. I feel I am yelling in the nightmare from hell.

The hardest thing in the world for me was watching the life oozing out of my dying husband in the car wreck that took his life and nearly took mine. The nightmare from hell showed in slow motion the deadly head-on car accident. It played out a tractor trailer driver falling asleep at the wheel. His tractor hit us head-on while driving in our new Cadillac DTS.

My husband, Rodney, died within a minute as I watched while in terribly bloody pain myself. We said we loved each other, and my husband of only ten years died as I blacked out minutes later.

I, along with my husband, died that night. I went through the tunnel, saw all the bright lights, the hundreds of whispering spirits welcoming me to the hereafter. But it was short-lived.

I saw my childhood spirit friend, Holly, who was also my lifelong, unique spirit guide. We spoke about my death, my husband, and the fact that I had to go back to my bloodied body.

"I don't want to go back to Earth. I need to stay here with my husband. I want death."

"There is a reason why you were put on Earth, Marjorie."

"I don't care to be on Earth anymore."

"While most people actually get to make that choice subconsciously, you are extraordinarily special. You may not fully understand this, but you are needed on Earth. You cannot stay!"

"Is this some kind of punishment because I have just been reunited with my departed loved ones? I need to stay here."

"You don't yet realize this, Marjorie, but your inner soul wants to continue to make a huge difference on Earth. What people do not realize is this: The soul will carry out the innermost desires of a human on Earth. In other words, the soul works around the clock, nonstop, to carry out what it believes the human being most desires. And your soul is convinced that you need to continue touching and improving lives on Earth."

"I have no options here?"

"You have one option."

"Great, what is it?"

"It has to do with me, Marjorie."

"You? What about me?"

"Well, your option is this: You can exchange your spirit guide, right now, for another spirit guide. That new spirit guide will remain with you for your full-term span on Earth."

"No way, Holly. I want you to remain with me forever. We have been together for so long. I love you!"

"I love you, too. But you will still be transported back to the hospital bed where you will recuperate…"

And that is exactly what happened. No matter how many times I dream about the horrific accident, it always turns out the same. The reality of it is, I was in the hospital for three weeks with multiple injuries. I had a collapsed lung, four broken ribs, a broken arm, lacerations that needed staples, and a severe concussion.

My recovery at home was long and hard. My physical therapy treatment went on for six months and was grueling. All along, spirits kept me busy, trying to get their own messages out to their loved ones on Earth.

For months, I slowed down by accepting new clients for readings. Valerie helped me every chance she had with driving me to all my appointments. The pain of losing the love of your life would be bad enough, but ongoing physical pains from such a horrific accident only compounded it all. Depression set in, and I had to fight through it all.

People do not understand loneliness and grieving until they go through it themselves. It may appear that a person is doing well during the waking social hours. But it is the lonely, dark hours that are the most agonizing times when no one or nothing can help.

Did I get to communicate with my husband in the hereafter? Yes, it was late one night and the most satisfying time ever for all of ten minutes. The message basically was, "I'm fine, we'll meet each other real soon again in

Paradise." The pain of losing Rodney came flooding back in my mind.

I even received a vision from the tractor-trailer driver who ran into us head on. He wasn't very sad over the accident, but rather matter of fact about it all. He explained while on allergy medication; he fell asleep just long enough to go out of control.

He did say he was sorry about my losing my husband, but he was very content with the hereafter. Most spirits are very content. Their sense of contentment results from their total comprehension of life, death, eternity, and the fact that life on Earth is but a mere drop in the bucket of time we all will have in eternity. It's as if life is just a very quick dress rehearsal for the actual play, one that is so long, so sweet, so perfect that most spirits can't even describe it enough for me ever to comprehend it at all.

I know it's a dream. I know it will end, but it goes on for what seems like an eternity. I try to will myself out of dream mode. I try to move an arm, a leg, even try to open my eyes. But nothing works. Nothing ever works when I am trapped in the nightmare. I know word for word, scene by scene.

When I ultimately wake from the pure torture, I am drenched with what could have easily been blood but is perspiration. It is as if I was submerged in a pool of water. I stare at the ceiling for a solid five minutes, trying to sort out the why of it all. Then sadness overtakes me as I relive the worst moments of my life all over again.

Is there a reason for such pain and suffering rehashed over and over again? I try to analyze the meaning of it all. Am I supposed to keep reliving the heartbreaking pain so that I value my life that was spared? Is it that the powers that be in the hereafter need to remind me that I was put here for a very special purpose, and I should not waste one minute of my time on Earth? Whenever I ask Holly, she merely says, "You will figure it all out one day."

Chapter Five

Carl Higgins was now one of my best supporters, but it wasn't always that way. When we first met years ago, Carl was very suspect of my claim to have communicated with the victims who had been murdered. Carl, a big man, black, 6'7" and over two hundred forty pounds, never believed in spirits, the hereafter, or much of anything he couldn't see. I won him over when I located the body of a five-year-old child who had been missing for two years.

The boy, Roger Contreras, communicated with me. He disclosed the location of his kidnapper and killer. Roger showed me the vision of the barn where his killer buried him in Iowa. He let me know his killer was an older man who had a plane and lived alone. Roger showed me what his memory of his killer's face looked like.

The killer was an overweight bald man with a scar on his face that ran from his forehead clear down to his chin. Roger told me the plane had a name on it, Nellie. With the help of Carl Higgins, my FBI agent the case was assigned to, we were able to track down the killer and dig up Roger's remains. We also uncovered the bodies of additional missing children. Gus Blazzell was a serial killer who avoided capture for more than fifteen years. Carl never doubted me after that incident.

"Marjorie, you never stop surprising me," Carl smiled as he welcomed me into his office in Miramar, Florida. The FBI building there is immense and very futuristic, almost as if it were a mistake to be built in 2018. I had visited Carl many times over the years for cases we worked on.

Once they no longer suspected my visions of the dead, the Agency learned to act upon my hunches and suggestions, quickly and without reservation, because of my successes.

"You know, Marjorie, not a day goes by without someone asking me about that serial killer Gus Blazzell case we worked on years ago. I believe out of all the cases we solved through your psychic abilities, the child killer was the best."

"Yes, the kidnapper and killer, Gus, killed five children. It was heartbreaking to visualize those young children and how he buried them. The families, though devastated at the digging up of their children, at least got closure in recovering their loved ones' bodies."

"I have to ask you because we never really covered this before, but, Marjorie, did you ever have any afterlife communication with Gus, the killer?"

"It is strange, Carl, but yes, I did have communication with the serial killer."

"My God, what went through your mind? Were you scared?"

"No, I felt very sad for the children who he killed and buried, for the families and for him. You are aware he killed himself in prison. It was the middle of the night; he slit his wrist with a shank made out of a toothbrush. It was a month after his arrest, even before any trial."

"Yes, yes, I remember he killed himself. I had forgotten when or how he killed himself. What did your conversation include? Was he mad at you for catching him and getting the FBI involved?"

"Carl, he was not mad at me. He understood all the things he did were wrong. He was sorry more for the families of the children than for the children themselves. He told me, 'You know, when I was a young person, I never thought I would ever harm children. I turned into a monster but never cared that I was doing bad. At the time I was doing evil, it felt okay for me to do it.' So why did I become that person, you may ask?"

"I would like to know what went wrong, Gus, yes."

"The fact that I was a monster only sunk in after I was caught. That is why I had to kill the monster, why I took my own life. I didn't want anyone else suffering. I didn't want a courtroom drama where families had to relive the vicious acts to their children all over again.

"Do I know now how bad I had become and why I slowly turned into such a cold-hearted monster? Yes. I have now repented for every sin I ever committed in life. I wish I could take it all back."

"So, Gus, I am very interested in what actually went wrong in your life on Earth. Why did you wind up going down such a destructive path?"

"I have carefully analyzed this endlessly. I believe that my abuse as a child had a lasting effect on me. We would like to believe that as we grow up, we could shake all the mental issues that hurt us early on. I evidently could not.

"I was beaten very often by an alcoholic father just because he was mad at trivial things, angry toward my mother, and because of the fact that he never really wanted a child. He was jealous that I received the love of my mother, and she showered me with much attention. My mother and I were beaten regularly. I believe it made me tougher and nastier as I grew up. There was unusual anger in me, inherited from my father. A wave of anger I didn't understand and couldn't control."

"How did you feel after killing a young child?"

"I felt terrible! Lower than low. I hated myself and would do harm to myself."

"Like what, Gus?"

"I would purposely cut myself and bleed, sometimes uncontrollably. I would bang my head until I passed out and even broke bones in my body as punishment. I would break fingers, punch myself hard enough to break ribs or wrists. I would do this for months, only to finally accept my acts of disgrace as acceptable. Then I would envision doing such despicable acts all over again. I knew I needed to die, but was too scared to kill myself. That is until I was finally arrested. I finally put myself out of my own misery."

"Gus, do you feel that you had a dual personality while on Earth?"

"Yes, now I know that there was evil battling good inside of me. The evil, of course, as I got older, won out and performed despicable acts to hurt so many."

"Any reason at this point why that may be?"

"I believe that evil was nurtured out of all the abuse I received early on in my life. I also believe that the evil festering inside of me wanted to get revenge on the world in its own way. Evil, I believe, overtook my life, and the good inside of me could not win the deep internal battle, not until I was able to die. The evil part of my subconscious mind willed me to take my own life."

"Why do you feel this happened?"

"It happened because the evil inside of me could no longer act out its aggression against mankind. It was finally disabled. The only thing left for the evil was to self-destruct. All this made perfect sense to me after my passing."

"That, Carl, was the communication I had with the serial killer, Gus. Did I hate the man who once lived and did so much hurt and destruction in his life? No. I understood what motivated this killer. I know now that he was powerless over the tremendous inner forces that controlled him."

"I never get over your awesome psychic ability, Marjorie," Carl said. "I don't know how you do it. I could never see myself communicating with all those different spirits. It really is wild."

"Well, you know, it never was my doing, Carl. All those spirits, early on when I was a little girl, sought me out. Why I'll never understand, but they chose me to communicate with. So, over the years, I sort of got used to them. They are very respectful of me, though sometimes they are somewhat intense in their need to communicate their story to me."

"Did any of the spirits scare you to the point that you wanted to break off all communications with them?"

"No, never. I'm sure there are mean-spirited entities in the hereafter. And what they do with themselves, I don't really know. But for whatever reason, mean-spirited entities never sought me out to share any stories. As I said, most of the spirits I have encountered have an intense need to communicate their stories through me and usually onto someone who is very near to me location-wise…"

Chapter Six

Carl and I documented the three-year-old death of Cynthia Green. He was astounded that the spirit of the dead woman came to me while I was eating just feet away from her parents in the Italian restaurant.

"So, you believe Cynthia Green was murdered instead of what was believed to be a drug overdose by the deceased herself?"

"Carl, without a doubt Cynthia Green was murdered, and by someone, she knew. She and her three girlfriends were supposed to go to a Taylor Swift concert together. Cynthia never showed up. But due to her bad ankle injury from soccer, her friends assumed she wasn't up to it. She instead wound up at Lauderdale-by-the-Sea beach with someone she described in detail."

"So, someone gave her the drug found in her system during the autopsy? Interesting! So, what else did you find out, Marjorie?"

"The killer convinced Cynthia to meet him in a bar. He then spiked her drink with a drug called Rohypnol. Cynthia had a bad ankle due to a soccer accident and was on Celebrex. Somehow, they made it to the beach, where she overdosed. She disclosed that the killer tried to rape her, but when she fought him off, he suffocated her. The authorities came to the conclusion that Cynthia overdosed because of the pain she was in and the mixture of legalized drugs with the killer's drugs."

"Okay, that is amazing new information. That changes everything, Marjorie. What else did she tell you? Did she say who the killer was?"

"Not by name. But she said it was a male in his sixties from the college. He wore a toupee and had very thick glasses. He was heavyset and had an accent."

"Not bad at all! That narrows it down for us. Let us open the investigation and start the engine up again. We will capture the creep; you can rest assured we will get him. Please tell the family that once we get closer to closure here, we will contact and fill them in."

"The family has suffered greatly for three years now. I felt their immense pain while visiting them. So, I will feel so relieved when you finally arrest this creep."

It was three weeks later when Valerie and I were invited back to Karen and Jerry Green's house. We were going there for an update the parents received earlier that day from the FBI agent Carl Higgins.

I had received ongoing communications from my lifelong spirit guide, Holly, who kept feeding me new information on other spirits and their desires to share their stories, but nothing new on Cynthia Green. The murdered girl suddenly decided to stop communicating with me. Was it because I handed over the information to Agent Carl Higgins from the FBI? Was it because continued communication through me would cause Cynthia's family much more added pain?

It broke my heart to tell the family that night in the Italian restaurant about my visions of Cynthia and how she was murdered. Though life in the afterlife was beautiful, and Cynthia made me stress that to her parents that night. Still, I was surprised all communication with her stopped, even while I was in her parents' presence.

Karen and Jerry were so happy to see Valerie and me on the second visit to their house, but they were clearly shaken up. Karen's eyes were bloodshot, no doubt from crying. Jerry looked exhausted, like he hadn't slept in many nights. Since we first met in the restaurant, Jerry and Karen had been on pins and needles waiting for the FBI and Carl to make some kind of arrest and charge someone with the murder of their only daughter.

We spoke about a few things first off, including Cynthia's spirit.

"Marjorie, we have been wondering non-stop since we last saw you. Has Cynthia come through to you with any new messages?"

"Karen, I'm sorry to report that I have not heard from Cynthia since that night in the restaurant. I admit that I am a little baffled. I thought the dialogue would continue, but I do believe that Cynthia wanted the next communication to come from the authorities. She knew that with the amount of information she conveyed to me, the authorities would have enough leads to follow up on."

"Is it possible that Cynthia is here with us now?"

"Karen, I believe that Cynthia is with you anytime you think of her. Anytime you say her name, talk to her verbally or in your mind, she hears you. Though she might not respond with anything you may see or hear or even sense, be assured she is responding in her own way."

"I believe that, Marjorie. I feel like my Cynthia is always there for me. We miss her more than words can ever describe. We do feel much more relieved after meeting you and your disclosing your communications with Cynthia. We now realize a hundred percent that she is always watching over us."

We finally got around to what, if anything, the authorities disclosed to Karen and Jerry. I hesitated to ask anything about it, though I believed the FBI had to get much closer to an answer in Cynthia's death. By law, the family must be notified first in any arrest, as it was their daughter. Carl did tell me that as soon as anything big turned up in the case, he would instruct the family to inform me as soon as possible.

Valerie and I spoke about going back to Karen's and Jerry's house for a second time. We promised each other not to fall apart no matter what was finally discussed, but I knew better. After all, how does one keep it together when the parents of their only daughter find out who brutally murdered the love of their life?

It was Karen who finally changed the subject to the Cynthia killing. She paused, looked at Jerry, then me, and then spoke. "Marjorie, Carl called today to give us a new update about the investigation into Cynthia's death."

Karen had tears in her eyes as she spoke directly to me. She also would look above my head, then back to my eyes as she spoke.

"You know, Carl has been working on Cynthia's case for some time now. He had called us weeks ago to assure us, after speaking with you, that he would not rest until the killer of Cynthia was behind bars."

"Yes, Carl is a great FBI agent and even a better person. He truly does care."

"Well, hours before we called you, he phoned us and told us they made an arrest." Karen now had her head in her hands and paused. Jerry moved closer to her and hugged her.

Just then, I saw a vision of their daughter, Cynthia, put her spirit arms around them both. Cynthia smiled at me and instructed me to let them know.

"Karen and Jerry, look at me for a moment, please." They both looked at me with tears in their eyes.

"Please don't move; remain still for a bit, if you will. Cynthia has joined us all, and, in fact, she is hugging you both this very second with her spirit. Cynthia is smiling and filling the room with love."

"I can see the light, now that you told us this," Valerie said.

"Oh, my Cynthia, we miss you so very much. Please tell her this, Marjorie."

"No need to. She is shaking her head, *yes*. You see, Karen, all you merely have to do with spirit is think your thoughts. They hear your thoughts loud and clear. Then you must believe that they accept and receive your thoughts. You may never receive a sign.

"I'll tell you a quick story if I may."

"Yes, please do," Jerry said. "Your insights already have been a Godsend to Karen and me."

"Karen and Jerry, there are so many misconceptions when it comes to spirits, here and in the afterlife."

"Here, Marjorie? I don't understand."

"Most people don't know this, but there are spirits all around us all the time. You may never see, hear, or feel anything from them, and though their physical presence may be very subtle, they are with you. Sometimes it's something as small as a slight breeze going by your ear or the slight touch of something on your bare skin. But be sure, Cynthia is with us now. She is very content in the hereafter; please be positive about this message from her."

"We feel so much more at ease because of your meetings with us. How much do we owe you, Marjorie?"

"Oh, please, there is no charge. The smiles on your faces and the sparkle in your eyes is real payment to my heart."

"You are like an angel sent from heaven just for us. You have no idea how much we had been suffering for the past years, not knowing. Now we at least feel like we have closure of some sort."

"Yes, I get the same response from all the family members after I relay messages from their spirit loved ones who passed."

"So, I'm so sorry, but I forgot to tell you about the messages I received for others."

"Marjorie, you are so interesting that I could listen to you all day. But I too must tell you what Agent Carl disclosed to us from his investigation," Karen responded.

"Well, I will make this quick. There is a message I received from spirit that was quite unusual. You see, I receive many messages from many spirits that had passed some time ago. But recently, I received a special request from a gentleman named Harold. What was so unusual about the message was this—Harold is still alive."

"Alive? But how? I thought only dead people could send messages," Jerry said with a stunned look on his face.

"Well, I will tell you this, Karen and Jerry. I almost dropped the hot tea I was drinking. This spirit showed up as a younger man, though he is currently age 47. Harold, unbelievably, is in a deep coma that will ultimately take his life. He was run over by a hit-and-run driver while he was training for the Boston Marathon.

"What he requested from me was that I seek out and speak with his wife in Galveston, Texas. He even showed me his home, his wife seated in the home at Harold's baby grand piano. He plays; his wife doesn't. But she was tapping on some of the keys while crying and thinking of Harold, who was in the hospital.

"Harold desperately wants his wife to know that he sees her and that he loves her very deeply. He said that he didn't tell her enough times when he was in perfect health. Her suffering with him in the coma is too painful for him. And though he knows he will be passing within a month to the other side, he needs to reassure her that it is okay."

"So, what do you do, Marjorie? That is quite a precarious position to be in."

"Absolutely. Harold keeps coming into my vision when I am at home eating, when I am driving my car, and worst yet when I am trying to sleep. There are times when we need to shut down all communications with the spirit world. We, psychics, need to recharge our batteries, so to speak, like all people. Harold just won't stop with the pushing. I had to tell him *no*. It broke my heart, number one, just to hear his story. But more importantly, I cannot play God. I cannot predict the ultimate death of a person that spirit finally entrusts in a secret vision to me.

"Death must have its own way of closure for the wife. God sometimes allows a person to pass over a given amount of time slowly. This, I believe, allows loved ones the chance to accept the inevitable passing,"

"I actually thanked God that my little girl didn't linger like that. Our nightmare was heartbreaking enough," Karen said.

"Yes, it must feel like the end of the world to lose a son or daughter. I can only imagine!"

"Yes, it is, but you have made our pain lessen a bit, especially by bringing Carl and me some closure to our family," Karen said.

"We all know that a parent is not supposed to have to bury their children first. That they should pass away before their children do. That is the most torturous event a parent can ever endure. I thank God that Cynthia came back to us through you, Marjorie. We love you very much," Jerry said as he got up and hugged me.

"But, Jerry, Marjorie knows how much we love her; she's a psychic!"

"Yes, I do know you care for me, and I feel so close to you through Cynthia's visions."

"Well," Karen began, "we were so relieved when FBI Agent Carl Higgins, updated us about the investigation into Cynthia's death. You, of course, were right on the money. It was determined that Cynthia never made it to the Taylor Swift concert. She never even traveled to the arena. Her cell phone was turned off because she didn't want to be disturbed.

"Cynthia had torn ligaments in her ankle from playing soccer. She was taking prescription Celebrex for weeks just to be able to get around. Now here was where you were right on the money, Marjorie. Agent Carl told us that Cynthia's killer was a professor from her college, Keisser University. The professor, Martin Bamta, wanted to have an affair with Cynthia."

"Oh, that is interesting. When Cynthia was showing me certain things, I was getting the distinct feeling that the killer was from the college, but it wasn't a young student but rather an older person."

"Well, of course, you were right. This professor was a single man of 62. He was divorced three separate times, had no children, was tall and very slim, and wore a toupee that was much too young for his face. We saw photos of him online. The FBI has documented the professor at the scene of the Lauderdale-by-the-Sea beach. The Beach Café's video camera caught him and Cynthia walking to the beach. Normally, the video footage is not retained very long. But because of all the alcohol they sell, they contract with a service that retains videos for five years.

"So, with that footage, the FBI issued a search warrant for Mr. Bamta's home. The home turned up incriminating evidence against him, such as items with Cynthia's DNA, her lipstick, makeup, and the bra she had been wearing that evening. It showed that Mr. Bamta downloaded child porn, and he regularly tried to lure young girls to his home."

"I see," I said, "So he is a child abuser too."

"Yes, he has been getting away with child abuse for many years, according to Agent Carl. Of course, they arrested Mr. Bamta and are holding him on a million dollars' bail."

When the evening was over, Karen and Jerry vowed that we all would remain friends for life. Cynthia came to me, once again, in a vision at the end of the night. She smiled and told me how happy she was that her parents were so much more at ease since the FBI and I were able to solve the crime.

Chapter Seven

I was exhausted, looking to fall off to sleep quickly that night after my visit with Karen and Jerry to discuss Cynthia's killer. But it was not to be. There are so many times when I need my space, peace and quiet, away from spirit messages. My spirit guide can usually protect me and my away time from spirit, but not this night.

When a spirit is so determined to get through to me, nothing in the world could ever stop them. There were spirits I had communicated with many times before. They each wanted to congratulate me on helping Karen and Jerry finally have closure in Cynthia's death. I tried to tell them I needed to get my rest. There were too many of them. That was until Harold Singlet appeared. The time was past midnight, and I knew I wouldn't be falling off to sleep for a long time.

Harold was the man who had been coming to me in visions numerous times to convey messages to his wife, Agnes.

"Harold, please, I already told you how I felt. I cannot help in your special request to relay information to your wife."

"You just don't understand! I will be dying soon! My wife, Agnes, needs to know that it's okay. Tell her I am at peace with dying. Can't you let her know this for me before I die?"

"Harold, I am sorry, but I cannot communicate with your wife while you are still in a coma. Your wife believes with all her heart that you will emerge from that coma and live a normal life again. You see, we as humans believe that God will always provide for us and answer our every prayer. We pray non-stop, straight from our hearts, and God is expected to comply with our desperate needs.

"You are expected to live, Harold. I will not go to your wife and tell her that you already know that you will die and that you are very content with dying."

"I see, Marjorie. I have seen the hereafter. It is beautiful, wonderful. I can't wait to be there. I have been given a special gift. I have been allowed to experience Heaven while still alive in my earthly body. It is truly Paradise.

"Do you realize that there is no hell?"

"No, Harold, I don't. Maybe that is because I have never communicated with people who would have belonged in hell. I'm just wondering, though, what happens to the evil individuals who do horrible things on Earth?"

"I was informed that they are forgiven. They remain in their own self-imposed limbo of sorts. They have eternity to make up for their bad deeds. Many of the really bad get to be reincarnated, with no knowledge of past lives. They may come back as the opposite sex or even a race they had previously despised. They might be poor if they were wealthy in a previous life, not knowing anything from their previous life. A second chance to live a better life."

"Harold, I will speak with your wife only after you pass. I am confident that you will communicate with me after your passing."

"I surely will, Marjorie. It's just that Agnes suffers so, begging God to bring me back, though my death is imminent. I need to tell her there is so much more after death."

"Can you control when you wish to pass, Harold? I heard that the soul can convince the body to pass away whenever it is convinced that the body and conscious mind no longer wish to continue with life."

"Yes, normally, this is true. What commonly happens, though, is the soul anticipates the need of the loved ones in terrible distress. It is arranged that the body hangs on longer than normal in such terminal conditions. It allows the loved ones in distress a little extra time to accept the ultimate passing of the loved one."

Finally, Harold was content with the promise that I would seek out Agnes after his passing. I would pass on to her all the messages he shared with me. I had to admit that he had some insights into the hereafter that I had not been aware of before. Most spirits have an agenda in their communications and visions with me. Most do not go in-depth about the hereafter workings, only that they are very happy. That we will all be reunited again, and death is not something that is to be feared or is dreadful to those passing.

The message is usually the same from spirit: "We are greeted, welcomed, and taken to the hereafter by our loved ones who have first passed."

But Harold had shared much more. He claimed he had knowledge that there was no hell. That even flawed individuals are not banned forever from Paradise. And even the bad ones get to be reincarnated and sent to Earth to do another entire life, with no prior knowledge of their previous lives. Amazing! There is no hell? Getting to do a complete life do-over? Forgiven of sins, except for one's own accounting and contemplation for an eternity?

Harold did leave me with a couple more secrets. He told me that a spirit, by just envisioning a place, can be transported instantaneously to such a place.

So, if a spirit chose to be on the Moon, they would merely think about the moon. But they also could be in many places at the same time. Harold said spirit could be in Florida, Italy, California, and on the Moon simultaneously. That was something I had never even imagined from communications with spirits for so many years.

Then Harold left me with one last thought: Learning in the afterlife never stops. If we can only imagine a genius on Earth, they are the most uneducated being when they arrive in the afterlife. The human mind can only learn one billionth of what spirit will learn in the afterlife. The learning is so vast that a human can't even contemplate any of it.

It was 2 a.m. when my sleep was again abruptly interrupted. I had only fallen off to sleep for a few minutes after my visit from spirit Harold. There was no sleeping for some time after Harold's vision and discussions. My mind was spinning like a child's top, uncontrollably.

I had called out to my spirit guide, Holly, but she was not responding when Harold's vision interrupted me. And she was nowhere to be found at 2 a.m. when the spirit came barreling into my brain.

I woke with night sweats and my head was spinning. The last thing I needed was another visitation from anyone. I always accepted the good with the bad in psychic life, but there are times that I truly wished I never had psychic abilities. It was amazing, but never once did I ever envision the winners of horse races or lottery numbers. How come I couldn't win millions of dollars by receiving messages where I could be rich? I often wondered if there could possibly be someone who secretly was being fed messages of winning numbers or horses ahead of time. That person, of course, wouldn't tell anyone about that special gift. No, my gift kept me up at night, unable to rest easy, unable to give my brain a break from spirits that had such desperate needs and requests.

Chapter Eight

I was fully awake, jolted from a deep sleep of minimal time. There was a high-pitched sound that made me uneasy as it demanded my fully awakened attention. The high pitch was more annoying than loud. Sometimes I hear a high-pitched sound for no reason at all. But this time, I knew a communication was the purpose of the sound. Once again, I tried reaching out to Holly to act on my behalf to keep all spirits at bay until I was prepared to contribute my time and full attention. Holly was nowhere to be found.

I wondered many times why Holly, my spirit guide, would not stand by me when I felt I needed her. Was it that Holly felt that these spirits, in those special instances, were in urgent need to be heard out? That no matter how I protested to time of night, my current energy level, or attention span, it was my duty as a psychic to acknowledge and allow those urgent spirit communication messages to be heard and acted upon.

It was then, quite suddenly, that the vision brightened up, and I saw the moving video. There was a bar, stools, floor. A heavy old wooden bar rail. Closer up now to where I saw the blonde hair of a woman. She had her head laying on the bar top, maybe sleeping, maybe drunk. There was no one else in sight.

Closer now, the vision showed the blood, the knife, the wound in the back, the slow movement, the moaning in pain. I was able to watch as this woman of indistinguishable age slowly died in front of my eyes.

"Why me, Holly?" I yelled. "Why do I need to see these things?" I was frozen in fear. My attention span was in full force now. It's incredible that the body reacts differently to different stimuli. My flight-or-fight instinct was in full gear, as the hair on my neck must have stood up. I was shaking, though I knew the scene was from the past. Still, I knew full well that spirit wanted me to see the death at this particular moment.

"But why me?" I asked out loud, knowing the answer before I even asked the question to no one in sight. I was needed. Spirit needed me to see, to know, to inform. I had the ability to hear from beyond. There are so very few with the expertise to listen to from beyond. I knew this, though I had learned that we each do have talents inside of us that will never come forth in a person's life.

There are people who were in a coma. When they awoke from the coma, they were suddenly able to speak foreign languages for the very first time. Then there was a teen who, after jumping into a pool, hit his head. The amazing thing, though, was this: When he recuperated from a head injury, he was suddenly able to play the piano for the first time. Not only could he play the piano with no prior experience, but he could play on the concert level. And now he plays for full houses giving concerts.

So, there are just too many things we don't understand about the human brain. We each have the ability to communicate with spirits. It is just inside our brain trying to come out. We just have to know how to flip the switch or flip one switch off and another one on.

The bloody vision I had witnessed of the blonde-haired woman dying continued. This time, the bar was on fire, flames shooting out from many areas. The bar was indeed totaled. It was so vivid of a vision that I thought I even smelled the smoke.

I knew then that I was in for an encounter with a spirit I had never communicated with. Why always murder? Why are women always involved? And why was it always so heartbreaking?

"Holly, can you see what I am witnessing?" I blurted out to an empty room. The room is almost never empty, though I asked for space many times from Holly. Spirits always are vying for a position to be at the top. They all feel that their needs are so much more important than their spirit counterparts.

"Marjorie, that woman was me," the sweet-sounding voice said. Then at once, the full view of the woman came in. She had long, beautiful blonde hair with bangs. She was slim and appeared to be thirtyish. Another senseless death, I thought. So many people are taken away from a full and healthy life way before their time.

"I agree," the voice came to me. "I was murdered, and I need your help, Marjorie."

"You know I don't specialize in this sort of thing. I am just a routine psychic helping people connect with their loved ones who have passed over," I tried to plead my case, though she wasn't going to accept my lame excuse to bow out.

"You don't give yourself enough credit. I know you can help me. Please allow me to tell you what happened," she pleaded.

How do you turn a spirit away? What could one possibly say to someone who was savagely murdered? I already had tears in my eyes, knowing this beautiful woman was taken away.

"My name is Julie Flanks. I was 32 when my partner and I were killed in the bar, the Red Light Lounge that we owned. My partner, Crystal Poreski, was 37 and beautiful. She was my best friend."

Suddenly I saw a vision of a woman who was stunning, with short red hair, green eyes, tall and slim, and also in her thirties.

"Yes, Julie, I can see her. She too, is lovely. Can I ask what happened to you both?"

"Crystal was from Las Vegas and lived there until she was 27. She was a high-priced call girl for a well-known mobster, Carlo 'Big Hands' DiLingo, a 6'3", 270-pound kingpin in the Litilio Mafia family. Crystal made Carlo a lot of money while working high-priced tricks for him. When she wanted to grow and run her own operation, Carlo allowed her to leave and gave her a loan of $200,000. She wanted to own her own business.

"Crystal relocated to Hollywood, California, where she still turned tricks. We met there when we both worked for an older woman, Madam Hilda. We soon became best friends, combined our money, and purchased a run-down bar in Hollywood, Bridget's.

"We worked hard over the years, finally paid Carlo back all of his original loan and many thousands of dollars of insane interest the mafia charges.

"Our bar was thriving. Crystal and I were only turning tricks for select high-profile Johns for mega dollars. But Carlo wouldn't go away. He kept coming back for more protection money through his local mobster soldiers. He was relentless. Carlo felt we had to pay forever, and we owed him twenty-five percent more each year. We finally refused to pay him and threatened to go to the authorities.

"That was the beginning of the end. He made it really rough on our customers and us. He sent goons to rough up our best customers and broke down parts of the bar. Our business fell off sharply. We couldn't pay our bills. A few of our customers put one of Carlo's goons in the hospital.

"That was one week before his goon took it upon himself to kill us both and set the bar on fire. The authorities determined that it was a robbery gone bad and never arrested anyone. You saw my body. Crystal was killed at her desk in the office. It was after closing on a late Monday night. They slit her throat."

"My God, I'm so sorry for you and your family, Julie. Do you know who it was?"

"All I know is the man is a soldier in Carlo DiLingo's Mafia family. He said his best friend was the goon that was put in the hospital. The goon has some brain damage because someone in our bar hit him with a bat. He said he wanted revenge, and although Carlo didn't order a hit, we wouldn't be missed because we no longer were of any value to the Litilio Family.

"I begged for our lives, but he kept saying, 'This is for Rocky,' his friend."

"Do you remember what this killer looked like?"

"He was huge, possibly 6'5" and 300 pounds. He wasn't young, maybe 60, clean-shaven, and wore a patch over one eye. He did say, 'I'll see you in hell, sweetie, 'cause you definitely are going to hell for screwing everyone for money. I kill people, and I don't care if I go to hell. It can't be worse than this cut-throat world!'"

"So, the mafia boss didn't order this killing?"

"No, Carlo would never have had us killed. Crystal and Carlo were lovers for a very short time, and though he shook us down for every penny he could get, 'It was business,' he always told us. He said, 'It's nothing more than business.'

"Marjorie, his Mafia family was in financial ruins due to the crackdown by the authorities against illegal gambling, drugs, and prostitution that the mob made so much off of."

"So, this Mafia soldier, working on his own, kills you both. Carlo did not order it, and it is made to look like a robbery."

"Yes. In fact, the liquor was taken, the money in our office was stolen, so the police chalked it up to a robbery-homicide."

"So, you want me to try and find this mobster?"

"We need to stop this madman before he kills others. I know you have special connections in law enforcement."

"What else can you tell me about this man?"

"Only that he lives in Hollywood, California, and drives an Eldorado Biarritz, red in color, from 1970, a classic. We've seen it around the neighborhood many times. He deals drugs and does illegal gambling in the streets around the area there."

Suddenly, Julie was gone. Nothing was shared about her family; no requests to contact her mother, father, or anyone else. Just find and convict this mobster who was nameless at that point.

There was no sleeping that night. It was as if I was injected with adrenalin shots. I was more hyper than I could ever remember. There were no more visits that night from spirits. Holly never even came to me, though I had been pleading all night for her assistance and guidance. No doubt, Holly wanted Julie's vision to play out as it did without interruption or my asking to be relieved of communication with Julie at all that evening. Holly, in her own way, knows how to protect me, though at times, I am convinced that she is just throwing me to the wolves.

I would need to disclose the full communication from Julie to Agent Carl in the morning. Julie's and Crystal's murders should never have been written off so easily. There are so many murders each year. But at times, it just is convenient to close the case, saying murder due to robbery and a fire destroyed all evidence. Next case, let's move on.

Chapter Nine

I was at Carl Higgins' FBI office at 11:00 Monday morning. The weather in Miramar, Florida, was steamy hot, already 95 degrees. There had been a drought, and everything was bone dry. Global warming must be the reason for the fact that Florida keeps breaking previous heat records.

Carl was intrigued by the Red Light Lounge double murder case. Valerie, my best friend and close assistant, accompanied me on this latest trip to see Agent Carl.

Carl had a file already on the Lounge fire and murder. He was on the edge of his seat when I mentioned Julie Flanks and her spirit communicating with me.

"What exactly did Flanks tell you? Because the investigation report disclosed that it is unsolved, a robbery gone wrong. There were no suspects and no witnesses. The case remains unsolved."

"Julie told me that a soldier in the Litilio Mafia family, in retaliation for a friend who had been put in the hospital from a fight in the bar, killed Julie and Crystal. He took it upon himself without the blessing of the Don, Carlo DiLingo, according to Julie."

"So, we have to look into the Litilio Mafia family for one of the made men?"

"According to Julie, he was quite unique-looking, acted alone, and was ruthless. There was no bargaining with him as he slit Crystal's throat."

"So, describe as best you can what this guy looks like and anything else we can use to eliminate him from society."

"Carl, Julie was quite specific about what this guy looks like. Though he didn't frequent the bar because the other goon that wound up in the hospital did, he was seen often in the neighborhood."

"Hold it there a second. Tell me about the fight and the goon that went to the hospital."

"She told me that Carlo DiLingo, who once had a relationship with Crystal when she lived in Vegas, constantly shook the two down for protection money, even after they paid back in full an old private loan.

"The women could no longer pay the increasing protection money, which was putting them out of business. The goon would come in, intimidate them, start fights and break up the place, trying to chase away business."

"Strong arming them!"

"Is that the phrase they use here?"

"That and many others."

"Guess us Brits aren't with the lingo yet?"

"Some of it you don't ever want to know. But, please continue, Marjorie."

"Julie said that man was in his late fifties, a huge man, maybe 6'5", 300 pounds. His head was clean-shaven, and he wore a patch over one eye."

"Interesting, Marjorie," he said as he rapidly jotted down notes. "Anything else?"

"Let me see," I said as I hesitated for several seconds. "Oh, yes, there it is. It is known in the neighborhood of the bar that the man is frequently seen driving a 1970 Eldorado Biarritz convertible."

"Wow, that is a classic car! I always admired that car whenever I saw one years ago. They are scarce nowadays. That would make this goon stand out from many others for sure. Anything else you can tell me?"

"Only this. Julie was very specific that the mafia kingpin, Carlo, wouldn't have had them killed because of the once-special relationship he and Crystal had while in Vegas. And the killer specifically stated that 'Because someone in your bar hit my best friend in the head with a baseball bat, causing brain damage, this is in retaliation for that.'"

"Okay, so we have so much to go on here. This should make it so much easier to close in on him."

Carl had a distant look on his face. It was clear that he was deep in thought. This often happens when people are in my presence. People know that I communicate with spirits, so they automatically just start thinking about everyone they ever have known that passed over.

Carl was lost in thought, and I could see his eyes suddenly get very moist.

"Marjorie, I hate to change the subject," he began.

They all say the same thing because they don't know how to go about asking me to request answers from a specific deceased loved one's spirit. They are afraid to admit openly that they believe there are spirits they can receive messages from.

"Carl, what is on your mind? Maybe I can help you."

"Oh, maybe it's nothing, Marjorie. I was just thinking of something from my past."

"I see. Perhaps I can intercede on your part. Is it someone close to you?"

"It's not exactly like that. It was a work-related situation. A person just came to mind. She died, and I was hoping to see if she was settled in the hereafter."

"The person worked with you somewhere?"

"Yes, she was an FBI agent. She died on the job."

"Okay. What was her name, Carl?"

"Roxie Dankin."

"I see," I said. Then I hesitated, waiting for a sign of some kind. "How did she pass?"

"She was gunned down, ambushed by drug dealers she was investigating for murder. She didn't have a chance."

"I gather all of this from Roxie. She says she knows how much you miss her. You must not feel guilty. You have to know that she is fine. The hereafter is much more than she ever expected. She says you keep saying that it should have been you that day that got killed, and not her."

"Yes, I am battling with that every day."

"Roxie says that you both had more than a working relationship. It was much closer."

"We were lovers. Yes."

"But you both were spoken for?"

"Yes. We were working on something that would have fixed that for the long term."

"Yes, she is telling me that."

"She is happy in the hereafter?"

"Yes, she says that. She tells me that you must move on, live your life, stop living in a bubble. You have much life to live."

"Marjorie, no one knows about Roxie and me, or our love…"

"No one ever will, Carl! Everything is confidential, always."

"Okay. Thanks."

"I'm getting something from her about eggs. Watery scrambled eggs, like soup?"

Carl laughed. "Spirit doesn't pull any punches, do they?"

"No. Why should they hold back at this time?"

"Well, Roxie is right. We were at a cabin. I wanted to make breakfast in bed for her. I tried to make my specialty, scrambled eggs and bacon. It didn't turn out great. I'm not a cook, and after trying to eat the eggs, her face told me I should keep my day job. Of course, we were both married then to other spouses."

"Yes, she communicated that to me too."

"We were deeply in love, Marjorie. I know that you probably are already aware of this from Roxie. It doesn't take long to recap one's history, does it?"

"No, Carl. It is covered quite rapidly by spirits. They can almost telepathically get all their important points across to a psychic."

"Well, honestly, Marjorie, when Roxie was killed in the line of duty years ago, I thought I would just throw myself off the nearest bridge. I was in a complete fog in my mind for an entire year. I was like a zombie, just going through the motions of work, life at home, being a husband to my wife, and a father to my children.

"I'm not proud of my behavior, but I will admit that I was praying each day that I would get into a face-to-face violent encounter with a suspect, any suspect, and kill or be killed."

"Carl, that is a stressful, painful way to live your life. Roxie is telling me right now that it was excruciating for her to observe this behavior you were displaying. She was confident that you would break out of that funk one day."

"Yes, well, it took, like I said, an entire year. There still is not one day that my heart doesn't ache for the loss of my love, Roxie. But I have, for my family, adjusted. I now am content once again with my home life and love my family more than ever before."

It was an extraordinary disclosure from my longtime acquaintance, Agent Carl. You believe that you really know someone well after a given time. But in reality, I have learned that we do not know most people well at all. We really don't fully understand their inner emotions, thoughts, turmoil they may be suffering through.

There are so many fighting through an inner pain every day. They struggle just to make it through each day. It's as if they are faking their way through each day as expert actors, and we are observing their award-winning performance as their captive audience.

"I'm so sorry for getting off on a tangent, Marjorie."

"Not to worry, Carl. I get this all the time. People have certain thoughts and emotions so deep in their minds; it is healthy to uncover them and discuss them. I'm your friend, and I will always be here for you."

"I also am here for you for anything. Don't ever hesitate, you hear?"

"Thank you, Carl."

Chapter Ten

The next morning, Valerie and I had breakfast—the usual oatmeal and two eggs over easy. Valerie helped with my schedule and breakfast when she was available. As one ages without a spouse, the close friendship of another is so precious that I would not know what I would do without her.

A ship in the middle of a lonely ocean, where the seas push an unpowered craft around, to and fro, is a sad way to exist. Valerie fills a void left with no family. Even as many spirits try as they must to make me feel useful to myself and many others.

We had an appointment at noon that day, arranged by Valerie. One day goes into another so fast, and weeks seem to pass as if someone sped the world clock up. There doesn't seem to be much downtime, though I am quite happy to be kept busy. A mind with too much time to contemplate dwells upon the sadness one tries to avoid in life.

Just as a performer feels so alive when on stage in front of a live audience, entertaining and receiving love from their performance, I need the love of my audience, too. I am on stage too. But I receive twofold the love, unlike a stage performer. Spirit fills me up with love, but it is the living, distressed individuals who suddenly feel reborn with hope and contentment about their lost loved ones that fill me up more than any love I had ever sensed before in my life.

So, all in all, I am blessed in my life, as tired as I am at times doing communications for the spirits. And it is an exhausting process as I try to decipher exactly what the spirit is trying to convey to their loved ones that feel so lonely without their presence on Earth.

"So, Valerie, who are we helping today?"

"We are reading for Mrs. Anna Downings. She lives in Atlanta, Georgia, with her husband, Thomas. She was referred some three months ago by Carol Galante."

"Oh, yes, Carol Galante. How is her husband, Carmine, doing with his treatments?"

"We spoke last week; Carol and I. Carmine is doing fabulous. All treatments are finished. He is clear of all cancer at the moment. They are delighted and send their love."

"That's so good to hear, Valerie. They both are very strong individuals. I feel so much love from the people we do readings for. They are so different after our session with them. So relaxed and stress-free, compared to before our readings."

"Yes, I also am so happy for the Galante's. All is well in their household. And you were a big part of easing their stress. You don't give yourself enough credit for changing people's lives. You touch so many lives on Earth, and then the spirits in the hereafter that you also bring a sense of peace to."

"Okay, enough patting me on the back. I'm getting a big head, Valerie."

"It's about time, my dear."

Our session began at 1 p.m. As usual, I know almost nothing about the person I am doing a reading for. Almost always, my readings are done over the telephone. People can't get over how easily I am able to connect spirits to strangers I have never met. As soon as I am speaking with a new customer on the phone, spirits come rushing forward, all trying to plead their cases that they should be first in line to communicate with their loved ones still alive.

So many people I am doing a reading for are stunned beyond belief when spirits coming forward are their deceased pets, or a newborn that died in the womb, or even days after birth. They can't believe that pets and days-old babies can have conversations through me, then direct to them.

Anna and Thomas Downings were on the speakerphone together. We spoke about the windy weather they have been having in Atlanta and how much damage had occurred, damaging churches and homes.

I waited for spirits to present themselves to me. Valerie pointed out the many orbs that were wildly circling the room. There were so many lights revolving, more than usual.

"Anna and Thomas, I am receiving messages from, I believe her name is Char or Charlie, or something like that. The woman is mid-forties?"

"Yes, that is our daughter, Charlene. We always called her 'Char' for short."

"Yes, I am getting that now. Char tells me that she is there with you throughout the day. I'm getting something like the refrigerator noise, and that it's time."

Anna is laughing on her end of the phone line as she says, "Char is right. We are way overdue for a new refrigerator. Our refrigerator is over twenty years old and is always being repaired. Now it's making banging noises. We want a new stainless-steel double-door model but have put it off for some time now."

"That makes sense to me now. Charlene kept making a 'bong' kind of sound. I hadn't a clue what she meant. That is the way sometimes spirit communicates to me, so often in riddles."

"Can you tell us if Char is happy where she is? She suffered so much while here."

"Anna, your daughter is quite happy and content. Charlene asked me to be certain to assure you that she is forever at peace. She is no longer in the pain that so tortured her, as you are quite aware, she informed me."

"Yes, Char was very sick. She suffered too much. It is almost five years since we lost our daughter to breast cancer," Anna said with tears in her eyes.

"It was a grueling three-year battle. It was very hard on us," Thomas said. She suffered, and while suffering, her husband divorced her. She was heartbroken, as she was without children. The three-year battle was the worst I had ever witnessed.

"It is most difficult to be able to stand by and not be able to do anything to fix the cancer. It broke our hearts those three years," he added.

"There are others who are accompanying Charlene. Do Annette and Charlie mean anything to you both?"

"Annette is my mother, and Charlie is Thomas's brother," Anna said.

"Well, they are fine and are standing with Charlene."

"Charlie passed due to a car accident. It was a hit and run, and they never found the person in the truck that killed Charlie."

"He has disclosed this to me. He also tells me that the man was drunk, as he was an alcoholic. He has since taken his own life out of guilt. He, too, is by Charlie's side there. Charlie forgives him."

"Oh, I see. We were so distraught about my brother's death," Thomas said. "Death always seems to change so much. Hatred sort of diminishes after the loss of a loved one who was killed. It doesn't make sense to hold on to a lifelong grudge. It is too draining, though we needed to know for all those years who was the responsible party."

The spirits were shooting around in my head, lightning-fast now, like a carousel at rocket speed. It was hard even concentrating on my conversation with Thomas and Anna.

"Are you all right, Marjorie?" Valerie asked, as she stared at my face. "You don't look well," she whispered in my ear.

"I'm fine," I lied. "Just a little overwhelmed with too many dueling spirits."

I spoke up to Anna quickly before all thoughts slipped by. "Anna, there are so many spirits bouncing around Charlene, but an older woman by the name of Annette is coming through, sending her love to everyone."

"Oh, that's my Mom! How is Mom doing?" Anna screamed into the phone.

"Annette is fine, Anna. She wants you to know that she is surrounded by all the relatives that have passed. She is always with you, hears your questions, and wants you to know that there is no reason for sadness for her or anyone else. Everyone will be reunited one day again; she keeps telling me."

Chapter Eleven

It was mostly small talk for the next half an hour that Thomas and Anna spoke with me. We covered a few more deceased cousins, friends, and uncles of Thomas' and Anna's. But I was only biding my time. Something was pulling at me. I felt as if a volcano were about to erupt inside my head.

The urgency was that great. No other spirit had that much pull on my attention and interruption into other readings. I silently kept asking my spirit guide, Holly, to help me. Finally, Holly came to me while Anna was still making small talk. I asked in my mind, "Holly, what is that intense pull on my brain? Am I going to have a cerebral hemorrhage and die right here while on the phone with a client?"

The pain was intense, and I tried to hide it, but it must have clearly shown on my face because Valerie knew something was up. She began to lightly at first rub my neck. And as she witnessed me relaxing a bit, she increased the pressure.

She whispered, "Get rid of these two. You need rest, now!"

I couldn't cut Thomas and Anna off. They were still very emotional, as were all my reading clients after communicating with their deceased family and friends. It hits them real hard communicating. Even though I am their conduit, all the emotions come rushing back.

Holly said with regard to all the spirits cramming into my brain, "Marjorie, I can't control these spirits; it's just out of control. All I can tell you is whenever spirits get this anxious, and out of control, it is urgent to them. There will be no stopping them until you hear them out."

After we said our goodbyes to Thomas and Anna and promising another reading in the next few weeks, I tried to sort out the other spirits. There were so many pushing their way to the top, trying to get me to give them the stage, front, and center.

There were cousins and grandfathers of Thomas' who were anxious to get in the mix on the reading. They were all bombarding me with stories about Thomas when he was young and played baseball for a minor league team. There was no time left. It is out of my control to appease everyone.

There are spirits that just don't want to understand. They all want to get into the act. They all feel that their stories are the most meaningful to the subject of the reading we are doing.

At first, I didn't want a reading to end. I wanted to accommodate every last spirit that appeared during a reading. Of course, over the years, I found it impossible to entertain every last spirit who presented themselves.

Then there were the jokers. It is hard to believe, but some spirits have no real connection to the person I am reading for, but they come through. Their real purpose is to have fun by making stuff up, playing jokes on everyone present. They are just spirits that, perhaps out of boredom, want to get a good laugh at fooling everyone.

It takes some time to catch on to the spirit jokers that interfere with some readings. And though it may be a rare occurrence, it is very frustrating for the psychic who is trying to mediate between emotional people dying to communicate with lost loved ones.

This day was no exception. I fully expected the persistent spirits that were hanging around at the beginning, during, and after Anna's and Thomas' reading, to be annoying jokers. They weren't. There was one spirit that shocked me to my core.

At one point, I lost my breath for several seconds. I must have become very pale because Valerie took hold of both my hands, looked into my eyes and said, "Marjorie, you are really scaring me now! What is going on here? Can I help?"

"Valerie, I will be fine. Trust me. It is just that there is such a traffic jam going on inside my head. It has been going on since the beginning of the reading for Anna and Thomas. Sometimes this happens, but this time it was very strange. Something very unusual is going on. Even my spirit guide, Holly, has no control over any of it. Sometimes Holly can turn it off, make the communications from the spirits cease. Not this time. I will be fine. Just stay close to me, please. We will need to have it all play out."

With that, the vision of a woman appeared in my mind, crystal clear. Other spirit messages and visions suddenly were overpowered by this new vision.

The woman appeared to be around sixty years old, slim, with long dark hair, high cheekbones, and very attractive.

Her skin was darkish, as if she might be of Native American nationality, but I was unsure.

She had a loving smile, and her eyes were friendly and dark. She made me feel at ease. Sometimes spirit can be, as with some people, a little standoffish. They can make you feel a little self-conscious, uneasy for several minutes. Maybe some spirits need to gather their thoughts, knowing they have to cram as much into the sessions of time, or it would be over for good.

Her name, she disclosed to me, was Theresa. That was all she would tell me of her name. She said that she passed a few years ago and had been divorced. She was insistent that I take notes because she was there to warn me if I was not able to change future events she was foretelling.

"I am here, Marjorie, because I believe you have the power to change a major event that will soon take place if nothing about the future changes."

"Theresa, I am basically a psychic that connects spirits of people who have passed on to loved ones still alive on Earth. I do not foretell the future, and I cannot by any stretch of the imagination change future events."

"Do not sell yourself short, Marjorie. You have advanced powers you have not even tapped into yet. You are only using about fifty percent of your psychic abilities at the current time."

"Well, I appreciate that, Theresa, but I do not wish to try and change that which is still to come. I am satisfied with using my current abilities to reunite loved ones. I draw on a great sense of satisfaction when a loved one realizes their family or friends who have passed on are content, safe, and happy in the afterlife. Why would I even consider future events?"

"Because if you do nothing, an airliner will shortly crash, killing all 100 passengers aboard. You can stop that event. I am sure of this. No one else is going to be able to stop that plane from crashing!"

"Oh, my God! But, Theresa, how can I possibly stop an airliner from crashing? I'm just an average human being."

"You are so much more. You are communicating right now with me. I had passed from Earth some three years ago. No one on Earth has had a two-way communication with me but you. You are so special."

"Okay, I will agree; I have a special ability that I have been able to develop. Others, too, have this ability, but they just have not developed it yet. Still, I cannot stop an airliner that is going to crash. What can I possibly do?"

"Marjorie, you have the ability to stop a terrorist act that a person on Earth plans on carrying out against an airline."

"Okay, you have my full attention," I said. Theresa was not anything but loving. She didn't try to intimidate me or force me into anything. She remained calm, which I was finding very unusual. She didn't come across as a jokester or someone out to make a fool out of anyone. She was as sincere as anyone I had ever communicated with, and as caring as could be.

"Theresa, how can I possibly save that airplane?"

"You will have to contact the authorities. I can't do anything. It is out of our control."

"Do you mean to tell me that in the afterlife, you cannot turn around evil like that?"

"There will always be evil in the world. If every act of evil were eliminated, the world would not have what is well known as *Free Will*. Free will has always been allowed to play out. Though, through acts of heroism, some evil acts have been quelled. You can save that plane, but it won't be easy. Only certain information can be supplied to you."

"Fine. I am writing this down," I quickly said.

"I know that. Remember, I am a spirit."

I laughed for the first time in communicating with Theresa. "Yes, you sure are. I'm sure you know everything about me, too."

"I do. And that is why you have been chosen, Marjorie. There is a person who will compromise an airplane at a New York airport. He is not affiliated with any organization. He is very depressed, distraught, and seeking revenge. If allowed to carry out his plan, he will ultimately also take his own life. The man has been battling this internal torture for many months. No one can change his mind for him. He will try to carry out his plan in the next several days. He has the ability and means to carry out such an act, and if he is successful, over one hundred people will perish."

"What are my best options to counter his efforts?"

"The best plan of action, which is not guaranteed, is to start with the FBI. You have someone there that you can speak with."

"Yes, Carl Higgins and I have worked together for a while now on cases. I can call him right away. What else can I tell him?"

"Only that a person by the first name of Andy is planning this act. It will be against an airline that takes off from a New York-based airport, and it will be in the next several days."

"Theresa, you have to give me more than that! How about the last name? An address, a description of some kind?"

"No. That is not possible. I'm afraid what I gave you is all I can supply. Remember, Free will. Catastrophic occurrences have been taking place on Earth for many, many years. They will continue, perhaps even more regularly."

"But we, on Earth, can't understand why certain horrific events are not changed, so they never existed in the first place."

"I will tell you this: There are many catastrophic and horrific events by very evil individuals here on Earth that never ever happen. Indirectly, just like with you, the powers in the hereafter work out the elimination of acts that will never happen."

"Oh, so you can fix mass killings."

"We encourage people on Earth to change only certain specified events, such as the one assigned to you. It is the people on Earth who actually stop some of the horrific events from happening."

With that, Theresa said goodbye. I asked more questions to no one there any longer. Questions never have to be spoken out loud when communicating with spirits. I do ask questions out loud only for the benefit of those for who I am doing a reading.

"Valerie, I will be all right," I assured her, as she looked very concerned about me.

"I never remember you looking that pale and weak before."

"I'm sorry, but you were not able to hear my conversations with the spirit I encountered. But it was intense. I must call Carl Higgins right away. Spirit tells me there will be an airliner accident caused by an angry individual. We have to try and stop it now."

Chapter Twelve

Carl Higgins returned my call the following day at 9:20 AM. I couldn't sleep the night before; I had an airline disaster playing out over and over. It was like a sick movie, watching an airliner crashing and burning, knowing every person on board would be killed.

Why me? Why was this thousand-pound weight placed on my back? I speak with spirits in the hereafter, and I do well with that. But I cannot change major catastrophic events of the world. If I fail, if that maniac succeeds and destroys that plane and all those souls, I will never forgive myself.

Sure, I know that there are very sick individuals in the world. I know that I can't control the minds of sick individuals, make them change their minds. For the first time in my life, I felt helpless. I am used to being in full control of everything in my life. But suddenly, I realized that there was so much I couldn't fix. So many people I can't help, though I help so many each and every day.

"It is amazing that you called me, Marjorie. I was going to contact you. But you probably already knew that. How foolish of me; you are a psychic," he laughed.

"I am a psychic, Carl, though I feel powerless lately. I need your help very desperately."

"Not again, Marjorie. We still are working on the bar murders, which I wanted to update you on. But it seems like you have something more urgent."

"Carl, while doing a reading for a couple, a spirit outside the family was desperately trying to communicate with me. So, after the couple's reading, I allowed the spirit to vent. It was an urgent and troublesome warning from Theresa, the spirit."

"I'm all ears," Carl said, as the silence of the two seconds that followed seemed like forever.

"Carl, Theresa told me that we need to stop an airline disaster. A depressed individual will be planning to down a departing airplane from a major New York airport, killing over one hundred passengers."

"And you are sure of the validity of this insight into a terrorist act?"

"If you are asking whether or not this is a prank of some kind, I believe the spirit to be quite accurate in her sincerity and major concern about the possibility."

"Don't get me wrong, Marjorie. I don't doubt your insights and messages, but others in power will have their doubts. This is a very serious allegation and must immediately be disclosed to the FAA and aviation authorities. Is there anything else at all that we can pass on?"

"The only name given was Andy. He lives in New York. He is suicidal and depressed. He was planning this act for many months and has finally committed to going through with it."

"Why can't we have a full name, a date, an airport, and an address of the sabotage. Why can't your friends in the hereafter give you exact information to corner this slimeball?"

"She was very explicit about why they don't just snap their fingers and fix such a problem. Because we, as humans, have *Free Will*. They only intercede in so many genuine and large threats. And though we as earthlings intercede and reverse some catastrophic, deadly events, the spirits are credited with motivating earthlings to do so."

"So, you are telling me that some people receive messages from afar and then counter aggressive intentions of ruthless individuals themselves?"

"Precisely, Carl. We are the conduit of spirits. We are their arms to change what they intensely need to change."

"Marjorie, I will not bog you down with any details of the bar murders at this time. I must immediately report the allegations to the FAA and Aviation Administration. I will contact you in a couple of days and give you a report on both investigations."

It was two days later when I heard from Agent Carl. Valerie and I were getting ready to go to the mall at Lauderdale-by-the-Sea. There was a business expo throughout the mall. It was eight a.m. Valerie had just cleaned up our breakfast dishes, and I was preparing flyers for my psychic table at the expo.

Carl was brief, and he was clearly concerned.

"Marjorie, we have been investigating everything surrounding all the New York airlines. The FAA and Aviation Administration, along with the FBI, are on top of it."

"Do you have any good leads, Carl?"

"I'm afraid we have nothing substantial at the present time. We have had a few dead-end leads, which we followed up on, including a fourteen-year-old computer wizard who was earmarking one of the airlines for identity fraud through an elaborate software breach he had planned.

"We are relieved to have shut his operation down, but this doesn't address the much larger concern. This is top priority now and has all the top brass of the agencies all on edge."

"What if they can't find the madman before he acts on his plan?"

"Well, there are special safeguards put in place at times when we have threats like this and chatter of threats from foreign terrorists. You see, we allow the prep of the plane to proceed as normal, but we then move the airliner to another hangar for a new and independent mechanical inspection by a completely different set of mechanics."

"That sounds like overkill."

"We want overkill, and we make no apologies for it, Marjorie. We cannot afford to have any lives lost due to someone bringing any of our airliners down. In fact, other states have adopted our temporary safety exercises for the time being as a precaution. Do you have any further messages from that same spirit?"

"I am afraid do not, Carl. There is no additional information I could relay to you."

"Well, we will not allow any airliner in the sky without that second independent mechanical inspection. The president of the United States has even been briefed on this, and he is waiting anxiously for the latest updates.

"Now, before you depart for your appointment, Marjorie, allow me to update you with regard to the double bar homicide. We have some exciting news to share with you."

"Marvelous, I am so happy."

"Yes, we have insights into all the mafia families in the entire country. Our offices are constantly following all the families. So, we go backwards and work our way forward. You see, the fella that got beat over the head with the bat at the Red Light Lounge, we started with him. You were right. The neighborhood knows him.

"He is Charlie, 'the Hat' Davies, also a soldier in the Litilio mob family. Charlie does, as you stated, have some brain trauma. We did question him and, though he wouldn't rat anyone out, he did acknowledge that he is best friends with the Cadillac owner.

"Eugene Filio, better known as 'Gimp,' because he has a bad limp from the service, is the friend and our man. We have video surveillance that places Eugene and his classic Cadillac at the location and at the time of the murders. There is a Bank of America branch doors away from the scene of the crime. Without your vision messages, we would never have known what car to be on the lookout for."

"Yes, that man did also have a limp. I might have forgotten to tell you that part."

"Not to worry. We have all the goods on 'Gimp' now, after we did a search with a court-ordered warrant."

"So, this person is the one responsible for Julie's and Crystal's murders?"

"Yes. We located the gun and knife used in the murders. They were in the Eldorado Biarritz, a 1970 classic.

Unfortunately, though, his arrest was not without incident. As he was coming out of his building in Fort Lauderdale, there was a gunfight with one of our female agents who was shot."

"Oh, my God!"

"Yes, but she will be fine. She was shot in the leg. We did apprehend him. He is in a load of trouble he can't buy his way out of. We will, though, need your testimony when it goes to trial."

"Sure, anything, you know that. I feel so close to those women. My heart is aching for them and for how they were killed. Life sometimes is not fair, Carl."

"Absolutely. When you least expect it, something blows up on you."

"Well, I've got to run now."

"Oh, yeah, one last thing, Marjorie. I feel you should know this. Eugene Filio is, in fact, not only a made man in the Litilio mob family, he is also the brother-in-law of the head of the family, Carlo DiLingo. It appears that Carlo's wife's sister is married to the murderer, Filio.

"Wow, that's not good news!"

"Well, all it really means is this: Carlo will hire the best lawyers for his brother-in-law. But he's dead in the water. Anyway, go ahead, Marjorie, have a great day at the mall show."

We said our goodbyes. And for a few seconds, I was silent as Valerie looked me over.

"You okay, lady?" she said.

"Oh, I'm fine. Just more to think about."

"Well, you look like you saw a ghost. And by the way, you're as white as a ghost."

Suddenly, I felt dizzy. I had to be at the mall in twenty minutes, but I was nauseous and light-headed. It was a terrible way to feel; when you become so unsteady, you feel like you will fall.

The mafia family, the Litilio family. Eugene Filio, the brother-in-law of mob kingpin Carlo 'Big Hands' DiLingo. In all the years I have been involved with spirit, with receiving and transmitting messages to loving and suffering living people, never once did I get involved in any way with the mafia.

I sipped water quickly, a few sips as if I had the hiccups. My head was starting to slow down in a slower spinning mode of dizziness. I ate a chocolate chip cookie, looked at Valerie, and said, "Let's go make this thing happen. Let's help someone out there feel better about life."

And that was what it was all about, this unique gift I had from God. At times I felt higher than a kite, helping people to finally have closure and begin to live their lives again, knowing their deceased loved ones are fine, settled, content, and are actually busily following the surviving loved ones' lives on Earth more closely than ever suspected.

The Business Craft Fair at the Fort Lauderdale Mall was a fine annual gathering of businesses and craftsmen who wanted to share their services with a crowded array of shoppers.

The weather was hot and muggy, and the temperatures had been in the nineties for what seemed like six months. The lovebug season was upon us for the second time this year. It looked like it was snowing heavily, but in reality, it was the millions of lovebugs in their final cycle on their way to their own hereafter.

There were tables strewn about all the corridors of the mall. Our table, entitled "Marjorie Chapman, Medium for The Living," was close to the food court. I was still not feeling well, but had to toughen up because people kept coming over to the table to ask questions. Valerie answered many of the administrative questions about cost, length of sessions, and what people could expect. I asked Holly, my spirit guide, for assistance in communicating with spirit.

But I soon had to get my act together as spirits quickly appeared to me as various people gathered all around the table, wanting to pick my inner mind about a deceased loved one.

I was speaking with a few people about future readings that we could arrange. A young pregnant woman named Gloria asked if her grandmother, who had passed, was in contact with me. I told her that at that time, her grandmother hadn't come through, but we could schedule a reading with her.

When an elderly woman with a cane approached my table, I immediately sensed a strong presence of spirit. There was a strong vision of a soldier dressed in an old-time army uniform. He was rather young. He came through with the name of Francis from Florida. I knew there was a special connection to the elderly woman with the cane.

She came closer to me as if she were instructed to speak to me. Her blue eyes were bright with excitement. I asked her, "Miss, does the name Francis, a young man in a uniform, mean anything to you?"

"Oh, God, yes. That is my brother. Is he here with us? Can I see him?"

"Yes, he is here with us. He sends his love to you. And he states that every time you think of him, he is right there with you. He sees you resting in your new La-Z-Boy recliner with the motorized remote control. And he laughs at how fancy life has become on Earth these days."

"Oh, I feel like he is with me when it is very quiet in the house, late at night, and I am all by myself, lonely, and sometimes scared of the dark."

"You are never alone; he is reassuring me. Someone is by your brother's side. His name is Robert. He is smiling down on you."

"That would be Bob, my husband, who passed over three years ago from cancer. I miss him so much."

"He says, 'You did it! You are stronger than you think you are. You are a survivor.'"

"Yes," she said, with tears in her eyes. "Bob always told me, while he was dying, 'You are stronger than you think you are. You are a survivor; don't ever forget that.' He kept telling me this while he slowly succumbed to the terrible cancer."

"Well, he says he is always with you, and to start cooking those amazing meals, you used to cook when he was alive. You are getting too skinny because you don't want to cook."

"He's right," she said as she shook her head, *yes*.

Then, as quickly as they appeared, her brother and husband disappeared. The loud sounds of a very busy mall were almost deafening. Trying to concentrate on spirits was almost impossible. Only the strongest signal from the most desperate spirits comes through in environments such as a busy mall or other noisy places. That's why it is most difficult to do readings in auditoriums or large gatherings. The spirit communications can easily cancel one another out and come through garbled.

This time was no different, garbled sounds in my head, visions like a movie reel playback at fifty times the normal speed. Everyone was staring at me, begging to be connected with deceased loved ones. It was almost too much to bear.

And then it happened. Clear as a bell; I heard her voice as she slowly appeared in my vision eye. It was Julie Flanks, half of the bar partnership from Red Light Lounge, who was killed. She was almost frantic with her message to me. Suddenly, the noise level of the busy mall, as well as the vision of all the shoppers mobbing my table, ceased to exist. Only Julie was in my mind and had my undivided attention.

Spirits can sometimes completely take over a medium's mind, eliminating any other thoughts, concerns, worries, or distractions from happening. This was such a time. Julie was trying to warn me about something.

"Marjorie, you must be very careful. There are people who dislike you very much. They may want to do great harm to you."

"But who? I see many people all the time. All I do is try to help people, even total strangers I see in the street. Whenever spirit comes to me, even in public places, I find the strangers and pass the spiritual messages on to them."

"I know you do. But the killer at our bar is out for revenge once he found out you were involved in getting him arrested."

"Wait! But how, who could have brought my name up?"

"Yes, but no. As I stated, we cannot disclose everything we are asked to disclose. You will find, in the world, many very tragic events, unchanged, that spirits could have made changes to. It is quite complicated, but suffice it to say that you must be careful. People are well aware that you were involved in the capture and detaining of the mobster killer."

As quickly as she appeared, Julie's spirit disappeared, and all communications ended. In fact, for the next several hours, there was no spirit communication of any kind.

I tried to reach out to my spirit guide, Holly, but she was unresponsive. It is a little more complicated than just asking for spirit communication and waiting for all the messages to come flooding in. If a person is under a tremendous amount of stress, in pain, or overworked in body or mind, then communications with spirit may be almost impossible, as was the case with my several hours of reaching out for some sort of spiritual assistance.

I discussed with Valerie the latest message that was passed on to me. She suggested I contact Carl, which I said I would do. But we needed to get through the day's mall show first.

We kept speaking with shoppers who came to our table, but no spirit was willing to come through for many shoppers requesting to seek departed loved ones through my assistance. We did make many appointments for future one-hour, face-to-face private readings. Our schedule was booked for many months forward.

There was a suspicious individual who was way off in the distance that was spooking me out. Maybe it was nothing, but it was weird, the feeling I had as he stared at me for a prolonged period.

I pointed the man out to Valerie, who tried to calm me down, saying he was nothing more than a spectator, curious that he would see a fabulous spirit communication from a famous medium.

Maybe I was paranoid about Julie's warning? Maybe I was overtired, as I hadn't been sleeping well at all? My mind had been working in overdrive, but I knew I couldn't slow it down. There were just too many messages.

I tried to look out the side of my head, being inconspicuous, as I looked at the man. Within a split second, I had a visual snapshot of him in my mind. He must have been fifty-two, of Hispanic descent, balding, and he sported a huge scary scar on the left side of his face, from his eye to his chin. At five foot ten, he was tall, but very skinny.

When he knew he had my attention, he pointed his index finger as if it were a pistol and moved his hand as if the gun was fired.

He quickly turned and left. Valerie saw this also, and she and I were clearly upset. This was no shopper or spectator. This was some kind of nut who wanted to send a message to me. Now I was freaked out.

By nine o'clock, Valerie and I were in the parking lot, loading the car with all the forms and flyers from the expo. That was when Valerie shouted, "Oh, no, look!" She pointed to the rear driver's side tire. "You've got a flat. Can you believe that?"

"No, I can't. I'm exhausted, and the last thing I need now is something like this."

"I know. Sometimes when you work your heart out, do great things for others, and give your heart and soul to others, the sky craps on you," she said. "But let's call AAA right away; they may take up to two hours to get here."

We called in the service call to my AAA account, and we retreated to the mall's restaurant, Red Robin. They claimed to have the best burgers in town. Valerie and I ordered the chili burgers, and I quickly called Carl at the FBI.

Carl had given me a special phone number that would be forwarded to him 24/7. I never used that number before. It took only five minutes before Carl returned my call.

I told him where we were, about the odd-looking man gawking and gesturing at me, and that suddenly I got a flat tire in a tire that was brand new, less than two months old.

"Okay, you must remain calm, Marjorie. That is the first order of business. I will place a call to the precinct captain in your county. I will request night patrol outside of your home, ongoing.

"You must be assured that no one will bring you harm in this matter. Once we have set forth an FBI investigation, the entire matter will be a much more important legality issue. If anyone breaks the law within the realm of our investigation, there will be extreme consequences to pay."

"But, Carl, this involves Mafia kingpin Carlo DiLingo and the Litilio family. How can you say that my life is not at risk? Let us be quite serious, please."

"My dear Marjorie, we already have evidence linking Eugene Filio to the murders. We have an airtight case brewing. Please don't lose sleep over a couple of disgruntled tough guys who will be arrested at the slightest misgivings. So please, let me go right now, and I will be able to communicate with the police captain."

We hung up, and our hamburgers came. I stared at my plate as if it were some kind of a masterpiece on display. I had no appetite for anything, and at that moment. My stomach couldn't tolerate anything that had chili incorporated within it.

Valerie begged me to eat. "You have to. You are starving, aren't you? Just eat a little."

I picked at some French fries, and they tasted like cardboard. It is incredible that when the mind and body are troubled, consumed with concern, food just becomes uninteresting.

"The food is great!" Valerie smiled. "You are just in a funk, Marjorie. You have to move on now, or it will eat away at you."

"But the mafia, Valerie. They don't play nice. They have guns, goons, and shovels to bury their enemies."

"Carl said that no one has the nerve to do you any harm. He has the murderer already behind bars. He has all the evidence he needs to keep that monster behind bars for good."

"Monster is the keyword here. There are countless monsters in the mafia, and they are very adept at intimidating, threatening, shaking down, and maiming. They don't necessarily have to kill you. They can torture you for the rest of your life."

"Please, now, you have Carl on your side. Carl will provide all the protection you will need. You must believe in him and the FBI. Please tell me you believe the FBI is sound and Carl is there for you."

"I do, I do, Valerie. Of course, after all, they are the FBI. They have always done well. I guess I am just very much on nerves. Even my spirit guide, Holly, had left me in the lurch, just when I needed some answers."

"Any reason why Holly is avoiding you of late? She has always been there for you since you were a young girl."

"Valerie, there are times when a spirit may appear to leave someone high and dry when they could be extremely helpful and supportive. What they are doing, in fact, is allowing life to play out the way it is intended by the souls of those living. Reality plays out, and spirit, for reasons unknown, must not step in to change or influence the scenes that were meant to play out."

We were called by the service technician of AAA. The tech stated they would be in our parking lot at 10:15. We were happy we would finally get the car back on the road, but as the service technician looked at the tire, he shook his head, *yes*. He was a huge black man who appeared as if he could lift the car all by himself without a jack.

He must have been six-foot-six and three hundred pounds. His head was clean-shaven, and he appeared to be around forty. His name was Samuel.

"Just as I thought, Ma'am," he said on closer inspection. "Someone clearly doesn't like you."

"Why? Why do you say that?" I asked, clearly upset now. Why does it always seem that when I try to get an appliance, my car or anything else serviced lately, the service person stares and shakes his head? Then the bad news is delivered. "Ma'am," they always say politely, "There is an issue here, bigger than first expected."

That is the announcement of a much larger bill they always seem to present. Plus, the time needed to rectify the unexpected, larger problem always takes an eternity with more problems that arise.

You would think that with all the spirits I have and continue to communicate with, I would get some special help from the hereafter. But, as I am so often reminded, "Free will must and always be allowed to play out," without interference from spirit, who may even want to rectify things here.

"Ma'am, upon inspection, it is clear to me that someone sliced your tire clear through!"

"What? What are you saying, sir?"

"Someone has it in for you. They sent you a message by cutting your tire, destroying it."

"My God, Valerie, do you think it was that nut job in the mall?"

"My money is on him!"

"Well, what do we do, Samuel?"

"Ma'am, this one is toast. Do you have a spare?"

"Sure, in the trunk."

"Well, I'll have you up and running in five minutes."

"Thank you," I said as I dialed Carl.

When Carl called me back, I told him about the slashed tire. "Someone has it bad for me, Carl."

"It's a message, Marjorie. My suggestion is to lie low for a while, no radio interviews, no newspapers or television at all."

"You really think that I am that famous?"

"You are in my world. I will pass on this latest development to the chief of police there in your town. They will review the video data of the mall and build a file. Not to worry, my dear."

"Worry, Carl? I'm way past worrying, now! How can I sleep now?"

"Let Valerie sleep over for a few nights, and rest assured that an officer will be posted outside your front door every night. I will get this authorized to continue indefinitely."

Chapter Thirteen

There was no sleeping for Valerie or me that first night. We stayed up talking all night. We baked peanut butter cookies and gave some to the officer outside my house, along with coffee.

His name was Jack Krauss, a thirty-something blond, slim, good-looking officer with five years on the force. He was not very friendly, but with a very military-style personality who was very intense and serious about his assignment.

"Ma'am, you are my responsibility. I must answer to the chief of police about your safety, so don't expect a lot of small talk from me."

All the while he was speaking to me, he was scouring the area visually for anything unusual.

"Thank you, Ma'am, for the cookies. You didn't need to do this, but it is greatly appreciated."

He ended the conversation abruptly. In a way, I was satisfied with Jack's commitment to our safety.

The following two days at the mall Expo were uneventful. There were many new interactions with potential clients, and we were booked solid now for the next two years. There were some characters that caught my eye.

People begin to look suspicious when you are scared someone is out to hurt you.

I was looking everyone up and down as they came up to and passed by my table. I stared at way too many people, getting weird looks in return, especially from older gentlemen who thought I was putting a move on them.

Finally, Holly, my spirit guide, came through to me. Why she leaves me hanging out to dry at times, I will never fully understand.

"Marjorie, I know you have been in an internal battle of sorts recently. There is no reason to worry."

"Holly," I said subconsciously, as I always do with spirits. "Where the heck have you been? You left me to the wolves, and you never even checked up on me. Why do you do that?"

"Marjorie, my love, I am always with you. You must realize that most times, life must play itself out. I cannot step in at all times and interfere with free will. I can assure you that you are protected there."

"Why didn't you warn me that someone could be after me? And that this Mafia person was a real risk I should not get involved with?"

"Marjorie, I know you better than you know yourself. You may be scared in the coming days, but don't let that stay with you. You will be fine."

Holly was gone as quickly as she showed up. I always felt, because of my special connection to the hereafter, that I would get special compensation for insights, favors, special treatment of some kind. I keep getting reminded that there are no special treatments from the hereafter spirits. They may be inclined to help change events, tragedy, and death. But clearly, they are limited by a higher force than them to allow most things to play according to free will.

Chapter Fourteen

The next morning Valerie and I were preparing for our client of the day at the house. We had a special two-hour reading with a young woman who traveled all the way from Staten Island, New York.

Two hours is an unusually long time to do a reading, but because of the long distance from home, she took a double appointment. The readings are, at times, very exhausting for me. There are so many competing spirits trying to climb to the top of the communication ladder so they can get top billing with a client.

Valerie and I purposely know very little about each person we book for a reading. Sometimes, they try to supply background information to Valerie when they are booking an appointment. Valerie has to stop them, explaining that I do not wish to know any of their details because, as a psychic, I will, if fortunate with spirit, uncover many of the pieces myself.

It was 9:30 a.m. when Carl Higgins called. It always scares me when I receive Carl's call. I know he never calls to see if I ate my breakfast. I had to put my complete trust in his ability to watch out for my safety.

"Marjorie, how are you doing this fine day?"

"I'm exhausted for one thing; I keep dreaming of mobsters trying to shoot at me from under my car."

"That's a new one. I'll have to remember that one. Do mobsters try to shoot from under cars?"

"I don't know, but when I awake from the nightmare, I am perspiring so much I believe at first it is real, and I am bleeding."

"I'm sorry, Marjorie. Perhaps warm milk before bedtime?"

"If I drank alcohol, I would drink the whole bottle, I would!"

"Well, on another note, we have an update for you."

"You caught the weird guy from the mall!"

"No, not exactly. However, we do have an ID of him being in the parking lot. But unfortunately, we have no footage of him slashing your tire."

"Great!"

"We do have better information. There was a significant crackdown on airline security by the FAA and local authorities, as well as our FBI. Passengers can no longer carry any bags onto the plane. We have confiscated any object that looks remotely suspicious, far more rigid than before.

"We initiated in Washington, LA, Chicago, New Jersey, and New York. Once a plane prepares for takeoff, we have initiated a strict protocol for every single jetliner to return for a complete re-evaluation by a different team of mechanics."

"Wow, that is intense, isn't it?"

"It is an administrative nightmare. We have it all under wraps, so the media doesn't publicize it to the public. But it was going to get out of there. The backup of planes is phenomenal, and there are many thousands of pissed-off passengers."

"It must be affecting the entire country, Carl. How can it possibly be pulled off?"

"This order came from the top, Marjorie. The order was not to spare any expense or workforce. An airliner terrorist act is never acceptable, of course. But one life lost will never be tolerated at all.

"We will never be complacent again. Not after 9-11, and not when we have any indication that a threat is out there. We caught what we believe is the only real threat out there, but are still 100% vigilant with all departing planes in many states. But we got our man, Marjorie. Because of you, we got our man!"

"I don't know what to say, Carl. That is the best news I have heard in my life. So many lives possibly saved."

"Here is what we have: An airline mechanic, working for a smaller airline, Air Baines, out of Schenectady County Airport, went berserk. His plan, which we intercepted and shut down, was to have the jet, a 727, blow up out of the sky. He in fact carried out the start to the disastrous plan. This man cut into a fuel line with such precision as to not have the fuel line rupture entirely until the plane was at an estimated altitude of thirty thousand feet. At that point, the fuel line will have ruptured and the plane, in turn, fireballs and blows from the sky.

"His name is Andy Gomez, age 34, who lived at home with his widowed mom, Theresa Gomez. His father died at age 50 from cancer. But get this—Andy's mom, Theresa, died after a plane trip from California a year ago at age 61.

It appears that while in flight on her way home from the wedding of her niece, she experienced chest pains. Shortly after an emergency landing at an undisclosed small airport, she died from a massive heart attack."

"Yes, Carl. Yes, it all fits in place now. The spirit that tried to warn me about the airline disaster was Andy's mother, Theresa. I can see her now. She is here with me now, and she is smiling. Theresa is so happy that we stopped her only child from blowing up a plane."

"Okay, that is wild—a mother, stopping her son—the only way she could from beyond, through you. I am so happy this all worked out.

"There were 87 passengers on board, heading to Wyoming COD Airport. There is no connection to that airport for Andy to pick. The only thing we can decipher is this—perhaps Andy wanted to handpick an airliner that would be a little easier to corrupt rather than a larger plane with many more passengers?"

"Theresa is acknowledging now that Andy wanted revenge. Blaming the airline for killing his mom," I added.

"Thank you, Theresa, for saving all those lives. Please tell her for me," Carl said.

"She can hear you and see you, Carl. Spirit, I am told, can be in multiple locations at the same time."

"That is awesome," Carl blurted out. "This whole psychic thing just blows my mind. I wish I could communicate with spirits myself."

"You can, and you have. In fact, every time you think of a deceased person, they can sense every thought going through your mind that pertains to them. They are instantly with you, watching you when you are at rest or watching the telly. They are quite supportive of your emotions, rooting you on when you need it the most. But people are mostly unaware of spirit interactions with them."

"I can only guess that after Andy lost his mother suddenly to heart failure, he just flipped out, lashed out, as if his world ended," Carl said.

"That is precisely what his mother said. He was suicidal on many occasions after she died. She tried to help him from beyond the grave. She even appeared to him, but he ignored it all. It was like a cancer eating away at him till he caved, according to Theresa."

As soon as we said our goodbyes, I felt so much more relieved about the airliner threat. What a disaster that could have been for the families and the country. We didn't need another 9-11 type of event; we already have enough daily heartaches in our country from some individuals who have pure hatred running through their blood.

Theresa stood with me for a few more minutes to communicate her appreciation. I could see her clearly now, hand in hand with her husband, Craig. It made me feel so thankful that I can communicate with spirit and give back to society. I also feel extra special when I see spirit reunited with a loved one. It makes life here make so much more sense.

We were ready for our client's special reading of the day.

Chapter Fifteen

Our client was a woman named Maryanne, from New York. I don't ask specifics, as I am the one to provide details for the client. It is essential to gain the confidence of the client. Most are naturally skeptical, as they should be. It is not a genuine belief that spirits remain amongst us. We grew up years ago fearing ghosts as some kind of villains. Only now do most believe that possibly spirits are out there, as well as the larger belief in aliens.

"So, let's begin, shall we, Maryanne? Now, you are living in New York, I understand?"

"Yes," she offered very little, as most of our clients do. They want to give very little, waiting for the opportunity to contribute only after they are convinced.

I had, as I always do, asked for my spirit guide to clear the way for communications. And I lit my candles, as it keeps me calm and focused.

Suddenly, there were spirits trying to communicate. Sometimes spirits get very anxious as they try to get everything they want to communicate out right away. Spirits are nervous that their time would be cut short, or even worse yet, that their main message will not be comprehended by the medium communicator.

"Maryanne, does the date February 29th hold any meaning to you? It's coming through to me. And it is a leap-year date."

"Yes, it does mean something."

"Perhaps an anniversary of some kind?"

"No, it is a birthday. My husband's birthday."

"I have a vision of an individual now. They are telling me the name of Matthew?"

"Yes, that is my husband's name."

"He is telling me that he passed at age 32?"

"Yes."

"Matthew is very sorry for leaving so young."

"Yes, he died young," she sounded like she was sobbing.

"He is telling me he had a sickness that he couldn't control. He tried to work through it all, but it consumed him. Maryanne, did Matthew take his own life?"

"Yes," she said as she sobbed, "I'm sorry," she said.

"Not to worry, my dear. He is showing me a uniform."

"Yes, my God! He was a police officer."

"And he says that he left two children behind? He is with them every day, as well as with you, too. He is showing me a blue ranch home and an SUV, late model, silver color, that he says you did a good job picking out."

"Yes, it's a new Ford Escape, silver in color."

"Matthew is showing me the car once again; it is an attractive automobile, Maryanne. Matthew is showing me a military uniform. He is telling me that he was part of military Improvised Explosive. He saw three of his army buddies killed."

"Yes, that is true, Marjorie. Matthew was in the army. In 2010, his patrol was blown up. All the men in the vehicle died but Matthew. He had injuries to his leg and shrapnel in his back. My husband suffered from PTSD. He was 24 when that happened in his service in Iraq. He finished his tour of duty and came back home."

"Matthew is telling me to say 2013."

"Yes, that is when we were married. It was on Valentine's Day of 2013."

"Is there a police officer in your family?"

"Yes, it was Matthew. In 2012, he became an NYC police officer. He remained with them until his passing."

"He is telling me of a shooting as a police officer."

"Yes, he was involved in a drug bust that went wrong. There was a shootout where Matthew killed one man in self-defense. During the shootout, Matthew was shot in the leg and almost bled to death. He did recover, but suffered a relapse of PTSD. He took his own life in 2017."

"Yes, he is telling me this, too. There is a woman with a cane with him, an Anna Marie?"

"Oh, yes, that is my grandmother."

"She sends her love and wants you to know that she hears you when you ask for help and answers. And she is saying 'doll.'"

"She always called me by that name, 'doll,' as long as I could remember."

Suddenly, Matthew and Anna Marie were drowned out. There was another spirit that was coming through very powerfully. I was unsure what to do. I had an uneasy feeling.

I spoke consciously to my spirit guide, "Holly, why am I being shut out here? I need to get back to Matthew and Anna Marie. My client, Maryanne, has more time coming to her in her session."

"Marjorie, I have no control over this new spirit force here. They are coming through with such intensity that the other spirits cannot override that force. I'm sorry, but you know sometimes spirits can be very forceful in their need to communicate. I would postpone the current reading and pick it up again at a later date."

I had hesitated for at least a minute. There was total silence from Valerie, Maryanne, and me. Everyone was waiting for the next communication message from me, but I had none.

Would this new spirit back down and allow Matthew and Anna Marie to return and resume their messages to me?

There was no communication between Matthew and Anna Marie. I could delay no longer. I would have to cut Maryanne's session short. It broke my heart.

Her husband took his life. Maryanne was just convinced due to messages I relayed to her that I was for real, that her husband's spirit was communicating with her. The emotions, the pain, the questions are still unanswered. It should not end like this.

"Maryanne, I am sorry, but we must suspend our session."

"Marjorie, I don't understand. We are getting so many communications from Matthew and now Anna Marie."

"I am sorry to admit that the communications have ended quite suddenly, my dear. This often happens at times. There are other spirits that have come in very strong. Do you happen to know a woman named Virginia who passed some thirty years ago?"

"I don't believe that I can recall anyone that passed from that time named Virginia."

And with that, our session was closed down. Valerie stepped in on the call and arranged for another date, and credit to Maryanne of time lost applied to the new date.

Valerie said later that Maryanne was quite pleased and surprised at the reading. She had not expected great results and was somewhat skeptical.

I was hoping that Virginia would go away, but she didn't.

"I'm sorry to interrupt your reading, Marjorie," she stated as politely as possible. "But I have urgent messages that must be passed on to the proper people. It pertains to life or death."

Suddenly, Virginia had my undivided attention. I waited patiently, but heard the communication from Holly instead. "Like I have been telling you, Marjorie, there is no stopping a spirit that is so motivated to pass on a message. If they feel it is that urgent, they will wake you out of a sound sleep, disrupt a dinner, or interrupt a church service or even a wedding if need be."

I needed to find out what was so urgent with this new spirit, Virginia.

Chapter Sixteen

"So, Virginia, what could possibly be so important that you had to interrupt a reading of a woman and family that lost their loving husband to suicide?"

"Yes, I interrupted, and I am sorry, but you disclosed so much to the wife, Maryanne. She was delighted with the messages. She would greatly benefit from a little time and space to absorb and reflect on it all. But, again, I am so sorry."

"Well, okay, Virginia, I am here for you. Holly believes you need to communicate, and this is what I do. I help the living and the spirit life to vent and reach out beyond the hereafter."

"Thank you so much. Marjorie, I need you to get a message to my granddaughter. She needs to see a doctor right away. It is a case of life and death."

"I see, Virginia. I assume your granddaughter doesn't know she has a sickness?"

"That is correct. If undetected much longer, she will surely die."

"Can you tell me more about yourself?"

"My name is Virginia Seditti. I was born in Italy and married Angelo Seditti. We relocated to Brooklyn when I was 22. We had two daughters, Patricia and Filomena. It is Patricia's daughter who is sick and has no indication of the sickness. Angelina is her name."

"I see. And what am I to tell her if I agree to seek her out? You know I don't ever get into the medical information services and informing someone that they have a sickness they are unaware of."

"You must do this for me, Marjorie. You are the only one I can trust to reach out to her. You see, she has thyroid cancer. She will not survive if she stays undetected. This is my 'little muffin,' and I can't allow this to happen."

"I understand, Virginia. I just am intrigued at how you are able to enlighten someone about a life and death situation while so many others must stay undetected and die?"

"This is a very complicated question, Marjorie, though an interesting thought. Suffice it to say that each human has a soul that is very accommodating. The soul has the ability to reach out across worlds and communicate at will, instantaneously with other souls and spirits.

"The soul carries within it the ability to allow a human to slowly end their life. It also accommodates and can cure an individual and prolong lives. That is why some lives are extended well beyond age 100, while others die prematurely in their twenties, thirties, and forties. I cannot elaborate more than that on the subject. I'm sorry I can't be more forthcoming."

"You have given me much to think about, Virginia. I suspected the human soul was powerfully strong and versatile. We humans are a complicated species."

"More than you can ever imagine. Humans have much power they never ever take advantage of. You are fortunate that you learned how to take advantage of the spiritual aspect, something others have not even entertained. I tell you, though, there are so many other powers available that will never be uncovered by humans. Their minds are too closed to experiment with their minds to open those unchartered channels."

"It's as if we are infants for our entire lives; we don't grow mentally to anywhere near our potential."

"Yes. Now, please, if you will, I want to disclose to you the special message I need you to pass on to Angelina. I chose you, Marjorie, also, because you are somewhat familiar with the family. Angelina is married to Carlo DiLingo from Las Vegas."

"Wait! Carlo DiLingo, the mafia kingpin?"

"Yes, you are aware that spirits of people you know somehow find their way to your doorstep to seek you out."

"I am aware of that, Virginia, but usually acquaintances, friends, neighbors, not mobsters."

"Marjorie, you must help Carlo's wife, Angelina. She will die otherwise."

"Why me? Why not seek out her doctor, her daughter, her clergyman?"

"You are the only one, trust me. Much thought has gone into seeking you out. You have an exceptional and believable reputation for being a genuine psychic."

"The Litilio Mafia family already knows all about you and the bar murder investigation, Marjorie. I assure you that Carlo DiLingo will, out of respect, investigate what you tell him."

"I am scared that the mafia family will want me dead for the information I gave to the FBI. I can't contact the head of the mafia family. Why would they consider listening to anything I tell them? To them, the enemy?"

"You are wrong, and I can guarantee that your information will be accepted and duly acted upon by Carlo DiLingo. You may believe that the man is bad, and his past is not perfect, but the man has done so many good things for society. Please give it a try. Please save my granddaughter's life."

Virginia quickly disappeared, leaving me to stare into space. Valerie wanted to know why my face was white as a ghost and who I was communicating with. I filled her in about Carlo's wife, Angelina, and the thyroid cancer.

"You can't contact the head of the Litilio Mafia family, Marjorie. They will cut you to bits and put you into freshly made cement!"

"I know. But I have to do something. I gave my word to Virginia. I'm scared, but I need to do the right thing, don't I?"

Suddenly, Holly came through to me, and I could see her smile lovingly at me.

"Marjorie, I know about Virginia, Carlo, Angelina, the cancer. What are your thoughts?"

"Holly, please tell me what to do. I need your guidance!"

"I cannot tell you what to do here. My job is not to predict the future or change human free will in any way. But I ask you, what is in your heart?"

"Holly, if it were my sister, my mother, or my friend, sitting with undiagnosed cancer, I would pray that someone would enlighten the person about their condition so they could seek treatment. So, my heart tells me to let Carlo know about his wife as soon as possible."

"Go with your heart, Marjorie. Always go with your heart," Holly said, as she quickly disappeared. Spirit has a habit of shutting me down quite abruptly. I was starting to get used to it after many years.

They make their point. Then, by disappearing quickly, they allow their words to sink in. Does Holly have an insight to know the future? Does she know if I will be in danger, or will I be safe? If she knows, would she disclose that information to me, or is that even allowable?

We are so consumed in our society about life, the loss of life, and keeping someone alive at all costs. Even our elderly ones in terrible shape are not allowed to die, but medical technology is used, regardless of all costs, if only to extend life for mere weeks or months. Even if the quality of life is very bad, the emphasis is to save that life at all costs.

I am beginning to understand that in the hereafter, that philosophy seems incorrect. Because spirit and soul do not die but continue for eternity, the extended weeks on Earth seem to be a futile effort in the inevitable. In fact, I am learning that the soul of the very sick is already outside of the body while the decrepit body is not of much use on Earth.

Chapter Seventeen

It was very early the next day. We had just finished breakfast, Valerie and I. Though she is living on her own, Valerie and I enjoy having breakfast together. We also like to have many tea breaks during the day. Why should we be on our own when we can have a good conversation and company being together?

"So, did you make up your mind, Marjorie? Are you actually going to make a phone call? Are you very sure of what you want to accomplish, and shouldn't Carl know about this?" Valerie shot me many questions in rapid succession, like a machine gun.

"Yes, I am going to call the office of Carlo DiLingo in a little while once I stop shaking."

"Are you sure?"

"Yes, quite certain that it is the right thing. I would feel terrible if I did nothing, and the woman would die. I couldn't live with myself. After all, I am here to help others, am I not? I am not in it for the money. I made my mind up, Valerie, so don't try to dissuade me."

Valerie looked up the phone number for Carlo at his business, which we located on the Internet.

"Marjorie, his business is called, Done Right Window Manufacturing. He is the CEO and has TV commercials advertising the window company. He is quite popular in Vegas."

"Okay, dial the number, and I'll pick up the other line, Valerie."

The female voice on the other end answered, "Thank you for calling Done Right, Las Vegas' leading window company."

"May I please speak with the owner Carlo DiLingo, please?"

"What is this in reference to, please?"

"It is a personal matter. My name is Marjorie Chapman, from Fort Lauderdale. I am a psychic, and Mr. DiLingo will want to speak with me, I am sure," I said confidently.

"I may be able to put you through to our plant manager, Ms. Chapman." She was polite but firm in her response. She must have strict orders of how to funnel all calls received.

"Ma'am, you don't understand me fully," I said quickly. "I am a psychic with some very urgent news for Mr. DiLingo that he will be very interested in knowing. It is imperative that I speak with him now!"

"Ms. Chapman, the best I can do for you is to take a message and let Mr. DiLingo know what you have shared with me."

I had no way of going further with the secretary. There is a time when you know you cannot get what you want. If you pursue the issue and get annoyed, your chances of getting your message through to the intended party greatly diminish. I was at that point, so I retreated as pleasantly as possible, and gave her my contact information.

The woman promised that I would get a return call before the day was over.

It was almost five o'clock when the telephone registered a call on the screen from Done Right Window Mfg. Valerie was gone for the day, so I answered the call on the first ring, "Marjorie Chapman, how may I help you?"

"Hi, Ms. Chapman, this is Gus Fauci. I am returning your call to Mr. DiLingo. How can we help you?"

"Mr. Fauci, I am a psychic from Fort Lauderdale, Florida. You may not know of me..."

"Ms. Chapman, we are well versed in who you are, what you do, and what you did."

"Oh, you are. I am pleased. So, maybe you can realize why it is urgent that I speak personally with Mr. DiLingo?"

"You will have to disclose any information you may want to share with my boss. These types of calls are always forwarded through me. I hope you can understand, Ms. Chapman. Mr. DiLingo is extremely busy these days."

"What I see here is a classic bureaucratic corporate roadblock. What you fail to understand, Mr. Fauci, is as a psychic, I am privy to important medical information at times. What I am telling you is it is urgent that Mr. DiLingo speaks with me personally. I must disclose this vital and private medical information to him directly. Is that clear enough for you, Mr. Fauci?"

"Ms. Chapman, I am Mr. DiLingo's personal and business head attorney. And as such, I feel it is proper to disclose this information to Mr. DiLingo through me. Allow me to do my job if you will..."

"I cannot. You can do your job by having him return my call personally."

"We know what you already disclosed to the FBI, Ms. Chapman. You may appreciate now why you must pass all information through me."

"Well, that will not work. That is just unacceptable."

"Does this information pertain to Mr. DiLingo's immediate family?"

"Yes, it does. It is very serious. So, when he is prepared to call me, I will gladly disclose the information, but not before then. Good day to you, Mr. Fauci. Goodbye!" I said as I hung up the phone, rather perturbed at the red tape in doing a good deed.

Holly came into view in my mind's eye. "No one ever said being a psychic was going to be all fun, no work, and no downright frustration, Marjorie!"

"Holly, why, at least once per week, I want to quit being a psychic. I want to hang it all up, and I want the spirit world to leave me the hell alone."

"Well, you will never stop me no matter what you try to do, Marjorie. You are stuck with my pretty face for life and eternity."

"Oh, you know what I mean, you ancient spirit from Mars!"

"Yes, I know what you are thinking even before you try to convey it. I love you, Marjorie, and know you love me, too. But I know what you are saying.

"Life on Earth runs in cycles; the psychic world is no different. Just like the cycles of the weather, the brutal, nasty weather, then the beautiful warm days, and then the tornadoes. Life is like that. What you must do is weather life's storms so you can bask in the most beautiful and exquisite weather nature sends your way. I know you are well aware of this, my love, but it will get better. It always does."

"Thanks, Holly. I was just venting to anyone who will hear my thoughts."

"Understood! I am here for you, always and forever. We are specially connected. Just think of me, my dear, and I am with you."

Chapter Eighteen

The air was warm; the stars were shining brightly in a picture-perfect clear sky. I was outside visiting with my policeman, posted as security detail. Carl, with the FBI, convinced our police chief to continue my security indefinitely.

It looked like a tough job to me. All night, stay awake, stay very alert, and be solely responsible for another human's life. *The pressure that must be on that officer,* I thought. *What must be going through his mind,* I further thought. In any event, I did feel relatively safe with him there for me. I was thankful to him, the police chief, and, of course, Carl, who had my back.

Officer Jack Krauss had the patrol car running as he usually does unless he was patrolling the perimeter of my house. He quickly lowered the window and said, "Good evening, Ma'am. How are you doing on this fine night?"

"I'm doing well. How are you doing? It looks so lonely in the car."

"Oh, I am fine. As long as I am on the job, I can stay awake. But thanks."

"Can I speak with you a bit?"

"Of course," he said as he jumped out of the vehicle and opened the passenger side door for me.

I handed him a bottle of water and a package of Ring Dings.

"How did you know these are my favorites?" he said.

"They are on everyone's favorite list, including mine!"

"Really?"

"Oh, because I am English, I'm supposed to only like English baked tarts and sticky toffee pudding?"

"No, I, uh…"

"I am only kidding, Jack, really. So, tell me about your family life. Married? Children?"

"I'm married, but no children so far. We can't seem to have children. It's probably me."

"Don't say that, Jack. Just stay positive. There are so many ways. You can adopt, doctors, so much more."

"I know. We just are taking a break from the stress of trying too hard."

"Jack, I have good feelings about this, so don't stress out. All will be fine. You are aware I am a psychic, yes?"

"Yes, the Commander briefed me regarding your case. I believe he said you have a business and your track record is very respectable as it pertains to the criminal investigation."

"I have been fortunate. You see, I don't really try to do anything. What happens is spirits of those who have passed from our world somehow contact me. And they do it at the most inopportune times. I could be on a bus, in a restaurant, on a beach, or even sitting here with you."

"Wow, they just talk to you?"

"Yes, and many times they show me pictures and moving pictures, anything they can as long as they get their point across."

"Well, I don't believe in ghosts of any kind. I'm sorry to say, Ma'am. No offense."

"No offense taken, Jack. Most people don't believe in what I do. That is, until one of their loved ones comes through to them as communicated through me. Like right now, Jack, I have a woman in my mind's eye that just won't leave me alone. Does the name *Arlene* mean anything to you?"

"That's my Mom's name."

"Yes, I am getting the name Arlene from a young woman with long, blonde straight hair and blue eyes. She is calling you her son. At least one of her sons."

"I am an only child."

"Yes, you are. But Arlene is holding a very young child. She says it was her miscarriage prior to becoming pregnant with you. Mom tells me she passed away too soon from female sickness?"

"Wow, you are good. My Mom died at age 29. I was only five at the time. She died of cancer of the uterus. It was a horrible time for our family."

"I am sorry, Jack."

"Mom is showing me a home, a ranch. It is the color of a light blue, and I see a swing set in the back."

"That was our house. I grew up there for a few years until I went to my grandparents' home after my Mom died."

"Jack, Mom is leaving my mind now but wants me to mention something called *hair tie*. It is a good luck charm for you?"

"You are spectacular, Ma'am. Yes, that hair tie has always hung on all the mirrors in every car I owned. That is what I keep to remember her by, her hair tie."

When I finally left Jack, he thanked me endlessly and couldn't believe the communication with his Mom. I think he believes in spirits now.

We had a pleasant little talk. I know he appreciated some company. We spoke about his wife, Elizabeth, his mother-in-law, whom he is very close to since his Mom is gone, and his love for the job.

Jack is a very good person who is a little on the shy side at first until he warms up to a person. That is why first impressions are not always telltale about a person. Some need a little extra time to express themselves. We all have our own little quirks about us. Spirit communications were non-existent after Jack's Mom disappeared. I needed the break. Communications with spirit can tire me out considerably. Especially when multiples come in, or the link is not that strong, and I have to keep guessing what exactly they are trying to convey to me.

Chapter Nineteen

It was nine-thirty at night when I returned to my house, after speaking with Jack, only to find a message blinking on my answering machine. I quickly played it back in case it was Valerie. It was Carlo DiLingo's attorney, Gus Fauci. The message he left played, "Ms. Chapman, this is Gus Fauci, Mr. DiLingo's confidant. Please call me as soon as you retrieve this message; it is an urgent matter. My private number is 347-777-7677."

I called the number straightaway. It was nice that he went out of his way to call me back.

After we said our hellos, Mr. Fauci said, "Ms. Chapman, you will be most pleased that I passed your message on to Mr. DiLingo. He was quite concerned about the urgency of your message. He knows your impeccable reputation, and with that in mind, he will be pleased if you will speak with him."

"Yes, of course, Mr. Fauci. I would like very much to have a conversation with him. He can call me in the morning, let's say first thing in the morning."

"You don't understand, Ms. Chapman. Mr. DiLingo will pay you a visit tomorrow as soon as his private jet will allow him to arrive. He will be at your home around noon, if that is acceptable to you? Of course, he will pay you for your time, as do any of your present clients."

"I don't know what to say, Mr. Fauci. I would be content with a phone session at Mr. DiLingo's convenience."

"You don't yet know Mr. DiLingo well enough. You see, he takes matters very seriously, and he is a firm believer in looking another person in the eyes when they are speaking with him. He knows how to read another person. In his line of work, eye contact is extremely important."

"I can appreciate that. I will warn you that I do a reading person to person, usually without others observing."

"I will note that for Mr. DiLingo."

"I do have another concern, which I hesitate to bring up, but I have lost sleep over it. There was a man who was stalking me in the mall the other day. Then, when I went to my car in the parking lot, I had a slashed tire. Law enforcement suspects the man is part of the Litilio organization. I now have police detail outside of my home, out of fear."

"Ms. Chapman, I give you my word. I will look fully into the possibility that it was one of our affiliates. We will get to the bottom of this, and I will inform Mr. DiLingo. Okay?"

"I didn't want to disturb you about the matter, but it has greatly troubled me for days."

"No need to apologize, Ms. Chapman. This is something we take very seriously. Please allow me to respond to you tomorrow, as I will be accompanying Mr. DiLingo to your home."

We said our goodbyes. I thought carefully about what I reported to Mr. Fauci. Was I wrong in telling him about the man from the mall possibly being linked to the Litilio Mafia family? Were the mob and Carlo DiLingo already aware of the man's actions and slashed tire? Or possibly was it Carlo that gave the okay for the skinny man, Angel Diaz, to harass me into total silence?

I had no way of knowing for sure either way. But I will know for sure about tomorrow's visit from Carlo DiLingo. Carlo wants to see people eyeball to eyeball so he can read them better. I feel exactly the same way.

Just then, my spirit guide came into my mind's eye. She pops in at will, and sometimes not when I desperately ask for her. There are times I feel I need guidance, and Holly is nowhere to be found. I feel like I am left to make the most complex decisions of my life all on my own. Then, suddenly, without warning, she pops in, gives me all the love and nurturing I didn't really ask for, but she must sense I really need. I'll never understand it. Maybe I am not supposed to. Afterlife is such a mystery, even for psychics. We are not to understand it all, not until it is our time to pass from here to there.

"Marjorie, please be careful with your upcoming meeting. There are dangerous vibes I am receiving with respect to these people. Someone cannot be trusted. You could be at risk by accepting these people into your world."

"Holly, can you please be more specific?"

"I am very sorry, but I cannot tell you anything else, except you must be vigilant. We are not here to predict the future, only avenues that could possibly be traveled by some individuals!"

"Don't you know for sure that someone will be committing a murder or taking their own life? I thought you had a crystal ball in the hereafter?"

"Absolutely not. We may have indications of what thoughts are contemplated in some individual's mind, but those are only thoughts—feelings and impulses of a human change every few seconds. There are millions that contemplate suicide or taking another person's life but never ever act upon those strong urges and motivations. Human nature works like that; those individuals who strongly desire to die sometimes never really want to die, and their souls can distinguish the difference in thoughts and overpowering desires."

"So, people can actually will themselves to die or live?"

"Yes, absolutely! This has always been a fact. Most people are unaware of this tremendous power that lies within every single human being. How is it that a spouse dies very shortly after their spouse passes on? They will themselves to end their own life. It is their own soul that actually carries out their intensely powerful wishes."

"And, Holly, the soul can actually extend a person's life?"

"Yes, the soul, if given direct, compelling, and powerfully intense directions for a person to be cured, and their wish to beat an illness, will at times comply and extend that person's life. We have all witnessed this and been astounded that a person beats an illness against all odds. It is the will to live which is very personal and inner to the person, sometimes unnoticed and unobserved by people around them."

Suddenly, Holly disappeared, again without warning. I hate that she does that. I can tell she is gone. I can sense that the video-like feed ends, though I am still sending her continued messages in my mind.

So, there I was thinking about a mobster kingpin named Carlo 'Big Hands' DiLingo. The man had a reputation in the crime family of being ruthless. So, what do I do? I invite this mobster into my home, right where I live. Have I lost my mind?

Then there was one of his goons, Angel Diaz, a career criminal and part of the Litilio mob family, who was stalking me. So, what do I do? I, as they say in mob language, I "rat" him out. I inform the confidant of the mob boss. I may have disturbed a hornet's nest at this point. The man slashed my tire. Now, what will he do?

Holly went and scared me even further. So, what did I do then? I immediately called the private number of my FBI friend, Carl Higgins. Carl calmed me down, saying, "Marjorie, don't worry. We have your back. I will personally be there for you. I will be inside your home. I will also have another agent with me and double up on the police security, too.

"We have no current beef with the Litilio Mafia family, so there will be no trouble. But we will be sure to disarm anyone carrying a firearm and secure the premises, just in case. You never know of potential enemies of the Litilio family or Carlo DiLingo. They live a very dangerous life; someone is always vying for that kingpin title. You never know when there is a hit ordered on you. Well, it won't happen on my watch and in my state."

"Carl, you just scared me more with the talk about possible hits!"

"Sorry. Sometimes I provide just a little too much insight. Again, don't worry. Only the good guys will be having firepower."

After we said our goodbyes, I sat and had a hot tea. Sometimes I get lost in thought while staring into the brewing teacup. All in all, I had a great job. I thought. I get to bring together the deceased loved ones with the grieving living. I get to change peoples' future lives by improving their current grief that they couldn't previously let go of before.

Sure, there were heartbreaking moments when I had to relive with the survivors how their loved ones died. How much pain there was. How much pain there still is. I felt the pain they felt, though not as much. First the pain, deep and hurtful, then and only then, the joy of knowing the families will have a far better future. That is the real dessert for me. That is what it is all about—the reason I do what I do.

Chapter Twenty

There was no sleeping the night before. So, at five o'clock the following morning, I was up, once again, staring into the teacup, looking for answers that clearly were not forthcoming. But as fruitless as my staring and wondering were at times, it was quite calming. The staring, along with the hot tea in the cup, was most therapeutic.

When I looked out the front window, the police cruiser was there. Different officers relieve my favorite officer, Jack Krauss, each night around midnight. But how long were they going to stay outside, guarding my house and me?

I phoned Valerie at seven a.m. and informed her to pick up donuts and muffins for later that day, when we would be receiving Carlo and his entourage. She was shocked that a real live mobster boss was actually coming to meet me.

"Are you scared?" she asked.

"Valerie, I'm nervous, but not really scared for my life. Number one, we will have Carl and the FBI here for protection. Then more security outside our home with the police."

"But Carlo DiLingo. He has some tough reputation."

"Yes, he does, but he will be here only because of the reading and messages received prior. Don't worry, Valerie, everything will be fine. I am delighted you will be here to support me and help, of course, with refreshments."

"We are joined at the hip, like Siamese twins, girl. Don't you worry about me! I'll protect you all by myself!"

"Tough talk from a little woman!"

"I know. I've been shaking since you first told me. And I'll be shaking like a leaf at your house later. But I'm there for you."

"Well, shake it to the store for me now, will you?"

By eight o'clock, Valerie was at the house with enough items and assorted muffins to feed an army. We were as prepared as we could be, cleaning, arranging, fixing up the place. You would think that the Queen herself was coming to my home.

By around eight-thirty, the place was bustling. We had two police cars, four police officers, Carl, and another FBI agent, Samuel Wentower. Samuel Wentower was a very tall, slim black man with a clean-shaven head. He looked like he played basketball for the NBA.

The four police officers were outside the house, standing guard, looking for anything unusual in the area. Carl Higgins was the lead person orchestrating security.

Carl told me that any and all weapons would be confiscated upon arrival of Carlo "Big Hands" DiLingo and any of his men. I felt like we were waiting for the President with all the security in and out of the house.

We were waiting, all set for the special guests, but time was moving in slow motion. It felt like forever waiting for DiLingo to show up. I was getting very nervous. What if the spirit didn't feel like they wanted to communicate with me for the benefit of DiLingo?

What if they didn't like him? That can happen, I understand. There are times when various spirits refuse to communicate with a psychic because they don't like the person the reading is being done for, or they don't appreciate what that person represents to humankind. How embarrassing that would be.

I said my usual prayer I say to the spirit world, seeking guidance and help. I reached out to my spirit guide, Holly, asking for her assistance in bringing forth any and all spirits that wish to make their presence known.

"Marjorie, you worry so much. Allow the world to look after you. Spirit will always be there to support your cause. I am pleased you have protection on-premises. I'm sure everything will be all right. I just get a bad feeling about the people involved."

"You and me both, Holly. I wish we just did this thing over the phone. What if this Mafia leader doesn't believe the messages? What if he thinks I am a fraud, a fake, someone out to take advantage of him? I feel safe today. Or somewhat safe. But what about tomorrow? What about when I have to walk to my car? Will it blow up? You would tell me if I were on some kind of Mafia hit list, wouldn't you, Holly?"

"Wow," she said, "You really do have a vivid imagination, don't you?"

"I guess my mind is working in overtime. I just get carried away sometimes with fear."

"Well, stop it, please! I don't see into every person's soul, you know. I do get vibes of some kind with some souls. These vibes, believe it or not, are passed to me by the respective person's spirit connection."

"So, you don't know of imminent danger?"

"No, not really. Only thought patterns sent from concerned spirit acquaintances of the suspected evil thinkers. There are so many individuals who never act upon terrorist acts or acts of suicide, though they may contemplate them."

Suddenly, at 9:45, we could see out the front windows that cars were pulling up; there were two black Cadillac Escalades. As soon as they were near the front of the house, four police officers were upon them. The other two were guarding the front entrance of the house.

Carl, Valerie, Samuel, and I witnessed the patting down of the four men, including Carlo DiLingo, the attorney, Gus Fauci, Paul Lano, and Angelo Giunto. There were no weapons confiscated from the men. Perhaps there were guns in the vehicles. But the men were told to remain outside the vehicles at all times until departing.

It was Carl who opened my front door to Gus Fauci and Carlo DiLingo; the others all remained outside. Carl introduced himself, first to Gus, as the lead FBI agent. Gus was unfazed, as was Carlo.

Chapter Twenty-One

Carlo was a huge man, standing six foot three and 270 lbs. He looked every bit of the 79 years he was reported to be. His hair was white, but full and combed back, as was his trademark for so many years. For some strange reason, I instinctively looked at Carlo's hands. I know I shouldn't have. But because he was conversing with Carl on a friendly basis, I felt I could sneak a peek. Why did they nickname him "Big Hands."?

Then I saw why he was referred to as "Big Hands." His hands were unusually large. And as I sneaked a peak at his very rugged face, though old, I could see how imposing he is and must have been years ago. I could picture him—hands around someone's neck.

I quickly stopped staring at Carlo. Gus, on the other hand, was tall, not as tall as Carlo, but very slim and in his mid-forties. He sported a goatee and looked rather distinguished. He seemed friendly, but very businesslike.

Carl explained to Gus and Carlo that he was there basically because of my safety concerns. And "that there was a person out there that was a potential threat, in Marjorie's estimation." They were okay with the extra protection.

Carlo moved to me and introduced himself. "Hi, Marjorie, I am Carlo. I have heard many good things about you. It is a pleasure to meet you, my dear."

"Yes, and you, too, Mr. DiLingo."

"Please, call me Carlo. We are going to be friends. Carlo, okay?"

"Okay, fine, Carlo."

"And please, if you will, allow me to introduce my attorney and advisor, Mr. Gus Fauci."

I shook Mr. Fauci's hand, and we all moved into the living room. Valerie was busy in the kitchen, preparing drinks and sweets.

"I must say, Marjorie, I am intrigued by what you do. I can't say, as yet, that I am a believer in spirits of any kind. I have always believed that when you are gone, you are gone. And nothing else goes on. I do believe there is a God, of course, because no one else could have created all of this on Earth and in the world."

"That is fine, Carlo. I respect your views. I will, though, tell you that most people with your opinion will see things differently, usually after the first reading I provide."

"Well, I look forward to that."

Valerie came into the living room with iced tea, soft drinks, and desserts. After we introduced her to everyone, we had our refreshments, spoke some more, and got along fine.

We learned that two of Carlo's men were outside the front entranceway, conversing with the officers and the additional FBI agent, Samuel Wentower.

"Carlo," I said, "I am going to request that we have a private reading. It simplifies communication for me. Carl and Gus can remain outside for the duration if that is acceptable?"

"Of course," Carlo said. "You are the boss here. This is your operation."

We said goodbye to Gus and Carl for a while. Valerie retreated as well to the kitchen. When we were finally on our own, quiet for a few minutes, Carlo said, "So how exactly does this work? I am so curious at what the urgent message you have for me is."

"We must ask the spirit world to help us here, Carlo. Please allow me a minute to say a silent prayer."

My prayer to spirit is always the same. I basically ask for guidance and protection and only spirits that are appropriate for the guest I am performing a reading for. I start out with my spirit guide, Holly. I asked Holly to oversee the reading and help invite those who would be most beneficial to the reading.

"I can't believe that you invited Carlo, 'Big Hands' DiLingo, into your home. Really now, Marjorie. Aren't you scared?"

"Holly, I didn't invite Carlo. He merely invited himself," I said subconsciously as Carlo was just silently staring at me, very patiently. He was smiling at me, and all I could think about was, *I wonder whose neck he broke the last time he got pissed off.* I know I shouldn't think that way, but it just dawned on me.

"I heard that, Marjorie. Spirit tells me it was about twenty years ago, back in the Bronx, New York. The young man was stealing from the mob. I understand the man died, but not before suffering greatly," Holly said. "I told you he is no angel."

Finally, spirits, other than Holly, were coming through. There were a few men and two women, one of whom I recognized as Virginia Seditti. Virginia was the same woman who first informed me about Carlo's wife and her sickness. The women were coming in much more powerfully than the men.

Spirits, when they have urgent messages, will just bombard me with encouraging vibes to listen to their stories. Other spirits usually get drowned out, and like bad reception, can't get their messages through.

"Carlo, I have two women here. The older woman goes by the name of Virginia. The other woman says her name is Patricia Albuno. Do you know them?"

Carlo looked at me with a sly smile as he said, "Marjorie, sweetheart, you are the psychic. Prove to me that what you do is bona fide." He smiled a bigger smile that said, "Prove it to me."

"I see. Okay, I am getting the messages that Virginia is your wife's grandmother and the mother of the woman accompanying her. The other woman is telling me that she is Angelina's mother, Patricia Albuno."

"Yes, correct. Angelina is my wife. Patricia is Angelina's mother, my mother-in-law. She and Virginia passed away many years ago. So, what do they have to say? Do they speak well of me?"

"I am sorry to report that you are not their favorite person, Carlo. They don't elaborate here in this type of setting. They do say that they forgive you for whatever actions you may have done over the years. Patricia, though, is complimenting you for being an outstanding supporter and provider for her daughter."

"I love her daughter very much. Tell her that for me," he said with a very serious face.

"Carlo, they not only can hear you, but they can sense what is in your mind as you are thinking about it."

"Can they see my future as you hinted to when you told Gus that you have a message for me?"

"Carlo, please understand, we cannot predict the future. I am not a witch or anything like that. All that I do is deliver messages from the beyond. The spirits out there have insights that we cannot or are not allowed to see or sense. Carlo, the spirits are telling me that Angelina is sick. She needs treatment right away."

"You mean virus, flu, ulcer, West Nile?"

"No, Angelina has a form of cancer, Carlo."

"What the hell!" he screamed as his eyes bugged out, and he quickly stood up with his fists in the air. "Are you some kind of quack? You bring me here to feed me shit like this?"

I was scared and pulled back into my seat. Valerie came running in from the kitchen as Carl Higgins came quickly in the front door.

"Is everything all right, Marjorie?" Carl asked.

"Carl, I'm sure it will be. It just is some alarming news I had to disclose to Mr. DiLingo."

"Carlo, are you okay?"

"I'm fine! Nothing I can't handle here," he said as he slowly sat down again. His look was distant as he spoke.

"I'm sorry, sweetheart. Can we please continue?"

"Yes, of course, Mr. DiLingo."

Carl and Valerie retreated back to their prior locations. Carlo studied Marjorie's face carefully as he slowly moved away.

"Please continue," Carlo said as he spoke to the back wall of the living room. He didn't want to look at me, and I understood. He wanted the news, however bad it might be.

"Mr. DiLingo…"

"Please, Carlo. Don't make me feel more uncomfortable."

"Just give it to me straight. Can you do that for me?"

"Yes, Carlo, I understand," I said, feeling very uncomfortable. This man dressed well, spoke well, but internally he thought like an animal at times. It was the world he was raised in. It was a tough, cruel world that was dangerous. It dealt with greed, illegal money-making schemes, territorial rights, and ruthless revenge.

And here I was, telling one of the most powerful men in America that suddenly I feel his wife has a deadly form of cancer. Valerie was correct; I should be scared, terrified. Maybe I should have spoken to Carlo over the phone instead of inviting him into my residence?

I tried to choose my words carefully. I don't usually get into breaking this kind of news to a client. Usually, I disclose how a loved one died, was murdered, or how they feel in their afterlife. My hands suddenly shook, and I couldn't control them.

"Carlo, I am not a doctor, but I have been requested, though, to pass on to you, urgent medical information. Angelina has a form of thyroid cancer. The spirits tell me it is treatable."

"You can't be for real. My wife is perfectly healthy!" he said in disbelief, while his face showed a newfound genuine concern.

"I am being told more information, sir. The stage of cancer is not yet in an untreatable stage. They are telling me that the type of thyroid cancer Angelina has is in fact very treatable but must be fully diagnosed immediately."

"There are no symptoms!" he shouted.

"I am told that what you should look for as symptoms are any lumps in the neck, pain in the neck area, and possibly hoarseness in voice!"

Carlo quickly got up and said, "Please excuse me. I must make some calls and also speak to Mr. Fauci."

"I understand," I said as I rose up and allowed him to feel comfortable in taking a break from our reading.

Chapter Twenty-Two

Carlo DiLingo clearly is a man with a short fuse. A man who takes no bull from anyone, someone, who with one phone call can move mountains. DiLingo's empire is fat with much wealth. Did he believe the messages I gave him about his wife's cancer condition? Will he actually take it seriously or discount it as a bunch of hooey? But, more importantly, if I am entirely wrong, if his wife, Angelina, is found to have no trace of cancer at all, will he retaliate? Will he get Mafia-cruel against me?

Sure, I had Carl Higgins protecting me. I felt reasonably safe in my home, but anyone can be eliminated or shot up at will. I learned that years ago when Lennon, the Kennedy brothers, and Martin Luther King Jr. were killed. And then, even Reagan was almost killed. You can't put a person in some kind of protective bubble forever. Anyone that is a target and has a big enough price on their head can be compromised. I was no different.

I patiently waited for Carlo to return from his phone calls. When he did come back, he was like a totally different person. Carlo was much calmer. He had a troubled look on his face. He was clearly scared for his wife. I waited patiently until he spoke. He sat down close to me and looked into my eyes. The spirits remained with me, hoping he would take the warnings seriously.

"Marjorie, I am very sorry if I came across as rude or arrogant. I mean you no harm. I realize that you contacted me, not for any gain of monetary value or publicity. I now realize, after contemplating all you have said to me, that you are a sincere and caring individual that genuinely wants to help others.

"You see, I encounter people all the time trying to get over on other people. Some will stab others in the back in order to get over on them, all for the gain of the almighty dollar. I have built a shield around my heart, keeping these people, and many others, from affecting me, getting into my heart, and taking advantage of me."

"I understand that you, Carlo, as most people do, have your doubts. I am asking you to believe in something you have no first-hand knowledge of. I want you to believe in messages from the hereafter. It is quite a stretch for me to unload such devastating news on you and have you immediately believing it all."

"Well," he smiled. "You are one hundred percent right. Most people would not accept your telling them that their spouse has life-threatening cancer growing inside of them. Well, I am here now to thank you from the bottom of my heart. Thank you, Marjorie. If you ever need anything at all, no matter how big, I will move Heaven and Earth to help you. Just call me. I'll fly a private jet here for you if you need it."

"I don't do this for favors or prestige. Carlo. Rather, I get an enormous amount of satisfaction and self-worth by helping others to soothe their grief and inner pain."

I wondered why he had such a change of heart. I waited for him to continue.

"Marjorie, I called my wife, Angelina, first. I questioned her specifically on any of the types of symptoms you described: lump or pain in the neck and hoarseness. Angelina said she has been experiencing pain in her neck. And she did admit that she felt a lump in her neck. Of course, I didn't tell her about your suggestion of cancer, at least not before she acknowledged certain symptoms."

"So, Angelina shows signs as explained to us by spirit?"

"Yes, I am sincerely sorry if I was rather short with you, sweetheart."

"Carlo, I fully understand your reactions. It is extremely hard to suddenly accept that a spouse could have a life-threatening condition. I only hope you are vigilant in seeking a complete diagnosis."

"Of course, I already called my personal physician. He takes my calls immediately whenever I call him, no matter where he is."

I knew the man was powerful, but it didn't get more powerful than this man. I wasn't one to judge Carlo DiLingo. What is wrong in some people's eyes is acceptable in others' eyes. I was only there to perform a valuable service. I would perform the same service for a man on death row. I learned many years ago that there is good and kindness in everyone. Sometimes one must look deep inside another to find that good, though it may be almost impossible to find.

Carlo continued, "Dr. Simmons already is arranging for his personal friend, who is a Doctor of oncology, to diagnose Angelina and fit her into his schedule right away.

Dr. Simmons cautioned me not to overreact or get Angelina too nervous. He says if it is cancer of the thyroid, there are many options, and it most likely is in the very early stages. But he said, 'It is imperative that we attack the situation immediately,' that 'delaying could be very risky.'"

We hugged, and I had tears in my eyes. At that moment, this Mafia kingpin did not look like anything but someone filled with love, compassion, and goodness of heart. Our reading was over. Carlo presented me with a check for $2,500.

"Mr. DiLingo, this is not what I charge. I cannot accept the check."

"Marjorie, please do not get me annoyed. Please put the check away. You are entitled to that amount. You don't want to hurt my feelings, now, do you?" he glared at me.

"Of course not. I would never…"

"We have determined that your slashed tire could, and I emphasize *could*, possibly be connected in some way to my man Angel Diaz. Of course, there is absolutely no proof to our suspicion, you see, but since there was the video of Angel in the parking lot, I feel it only proper to include a thousand extra for your tire."

"So, this man admitted…"

"I never said that, sweetheart. Let's just forget it, shall we?"

"But I still think it is too…"

"It is exactly what I want you to have. And for Angel Diaz, we have taken care of him in our own way."

"You did?"

"Please don't let your imagination run wild. We were letting him rise in our organization, but have now stopped that. He will no longer be eligible to move up in our organization, ever!"

"I see. I am sorry for the man."

"Let us say our goodbyes for the day. We will be meeting again because you are now a friend." We hugged, and Carlo kissed me softly on both cheeks.

After Carlo left, Valerie, the FBI agents Samuel and Carl, and I discussed the DiLingo visit.

I told Carl about Carlo's wife, the cancer messages from the spirits, the symptoms, and his calls to his wife and doctor.

"You did him a real solid, there, Marjorie."

"Solid?"

"Yes, a tremendous favor. You probably saved his wife's life. I'm sure he appreciated that gesture."

"He does. He told me anything I ever need, I should just call him, and he will make it happen."

"He did?"

"Yes, including supplying a private jet to take me anywhere I would like to go to. Do you believe this man?"

"I do believe it. The Litilio family is rich beyond belief. They have profited from illegal activities for generations. We can't seem to make anything stick on him."

"He drastically overpaid me and told me unless I kept the full payment, I would offend him. I kept it. But I found it strange when he said that the man from the mall, Angel Diaz, would not rise in the family's ranks. He said there was a possibility that Diaz, on his own, possibly could have slashed the tire. But, of course, there is no evidence."

"You know what that means, don't you? Diaz was due to become a 'Made Man' in the mafia family. But now he will never be or is postponed from becoming 'Made.'"

"That is a great promotion?"

"Much more than that. It is protection from many things. It is money, much respect, and a lifetime connection to the higher part of the leaders of the Litilio family. Should we pick him up and question him, Marjorie, we may get him to admit what he 'did,' though it is fairly unlikely."

"No, please don't. I just won over Mr. DiLingo. He likes me now. I don't want to undo all of that. After all, the bloke paid me for all the damages and so much more. Leave it be, please."

"Whatever you want. I am sure Diaz acted on his own in that matter. DiLingo wouldn't lower himself down for such a trivial act like that. After all, he despised his brother-in-law that killed those women in the bar. He would surely distance himself from him, the killings, and Diaz. I don't think Diaz's act disturbed DiLingo too much. If it did, though, and he took a real liking to you, Diaz could wind up swimming with the fishes."

"Now that is one term I fully understand. The chap could be wasted, thrown in the ocean, and maybe have concrete blocks tied to his feet, making him sink?"

"Precisely. You are catching on quickly. Just remain safe and vigilant, Marjorie. Watch out for tails or anything suspicious."

"I know tails are when they follow you, but you don't know they are. I don't feel any danger now, Carl. I feel much better about DiLingo. I no longer feel threatened by DiLingo or any of his men."

"Well, just keep your guard up. And make sure you call my cell phone if you find anything out of the ordinary."

Chapter Twenty-Three

The rain was heavy, the humidity unbearable, and the temperature at seven-thirty that evening was still ninety-one degrees.

With one hand on the umbrella, and the other on a glass of cold milk and a Ring Ding package, I approached the cruiser. The wipers were slapping from side to side, and Officer Jack Krauss was listening to talk radio. Jack quickly jumped out of the car and held the umbrella over me.

"What are you doing in the nasty rain?"

"I come bearing gifts!"

"Come, get in the car," he said as he held open the passenger side door for me.

"This is a Ring Ding rainy night!"

"Every night is a Ring Ding night, Ma'am!"

"Milk and Ring Dings?"

"Now you're talking! So, how are you and how did you do today with your special Vegas 'Don'?"

"Oh, I am peachy! I'm as giddy as a fat boy in a candy shop, I am."

"Well, you are trying to fatten me up for something, Marjorie. What might that be?"

"Jack, you have no idea how safe I feel with you watching out for me. Thank you."

"Well, thanks for the drink, but for a week, you will have a new officer in my time slot because I'll be on vacation."

"Holiday? Good for you, Jack. Are you going to travel?"

"No, just going to chill out, day trips, catching up on projects around the house."

"When do you start?"

"Tomorrow, bright and early. A big breakfast at the diner."

"Good for you!"

"So, tell me how you made out with the 'Big Man.'"

"Carlo DiLingo is not as tough as he leads people to believe. He has a soft, lovable side to him. He is generous and fair. And he is punishing that Angel Diaz, who he believes slashed my tire. Something about not being given a raise in rank in the Litilio family."

"You mean, not being allowed to become a 'Made Man.' That is punishment for someone who feels they were loyal to the mafia family. He could be on the way out of that Mafia family or on probation, of sorts. Or, he could just be in limbo for a short period and be allowed to become a 'Made Man' one day. We won't know that. But our force is here for you, be sure of that."

"So, who will be the recipient of tomorrow's refreshments?" I asked him.

"Your personal security detail in my time slot will be Kent Logan, a young, one-year veteran on the job. He is a great guy, very good at what he does."

Jack, like the gentleman he is, walked me back to my front door. The pouring rain was making many puddles all around the property. The rain didn't faze him. he walked in it like the sun was shining brightly. I would miss Jack. We had great little talks. Once he got past his shyness, he was quite outgoing and forthcoming.

The next day was going to be a busy one. I was booked for two readings, which is quite unusual, but sometimes I will accommodate people and their schedules.

Valerie was in a rather jolly mood that hot, sunny morning. She announced she wanted to cook us omelets to go along with the hot bagels she picked up on her way in.

"I'm going to make us western omelets," Valerie stated. "You need to keep your energy up; you have a packed day—two readings and phone calls to make."

"Western? You know how much I like my western omelets. That along with an egg bagel, and I am good for an entire day."

"Well, you make some of those return calls and I'll work my magic in the kitchen."

I followed up on a few people we did readings for about a month ago. There are many times when I come up with dates, names, pictures of things that people can't readily place or don't recall at the time of their readings. So, they call me back when they suddenly can piece together details of things that during a reading they could not place in their lives.

After an hour of calls and three more clients satisfied with the details they finally placed, like a missing jigsaw puzzle, Valerie was then ready to serve our breakfast. As we ate, I wanted to review the day's scheduled readings.

"So, what is on the agenda, Valerie?"

"We have a couple from Hagerstown, Maryland. They have been waiting for a reading for more than six months."

"And we have another reading?"

"Yes, a married couple from Woodbridge, New Jersey, Crystal, and Gene. They have waited a year to have a reading with you for August 17th."

"Officer Jack is on vacation starting today. I'm going to miss Jack."

"I know you felt so safe with him. I'm sure they will assign someone just as good. And, anyway, now that Carlo, the mafia head, is on your side…"

"I guess you are right. Still, something is in the back of my head. I can't wait for Jack to get back again."

It was before noon before my first reading was to take place. I said my prayers to the spirit world, asking for guidance. I asked for strength, as the readings drained me terribly. There are times that I juggle numerous spirits, all vying for the limelight to get their messages accepted and passed through.

Then, when I see the pain across my clients' faces when they relive the final moments of their loved one's life, it is pure heartache for me, though I know it will turn around, as it usually does.

Most clients have a newfound sense of peace and calm after receiving loving messages from their spirit loved ones. We all want to believe there is a better place, an eternal existence after life on Earth. But I think most people have doubts, though they want to believe. Only after a convincing session with spirits sending compelling and calming messages, do they believe.

Suddenly, Holly appeared in my mind, as is usually the case before each reading in answer to my spirit prayers. Holly helps spirits to come into my private space. Part of the prayer each time is to welcome spirits that are connected to the clients into my home space.

"Marjorie," Holly said. "Please be careful."

"Do you know something? Please tell me, Holly," I asked nervously. "I don't like when you tell me things like this. Be specific."

"I cannot, Marjorie. I told you we get vibes of thoughts. Humankind thinks of many thoughts of actions and motivations that never materialize. I am only warning you to stay vigilant. Be on your guard at all times. I am glad you have security. That is very important. There are many thoughts in the universe about you, all revolving in soul form. So many of these thoughts are favorable. But as I stated, some thought impulses are negative in nature."

"I am scared!"

"Don't be, but ask for additional spirit guidance and protection. This can help you greatly in times of danger. Don't ever discount spirit power from the beyond. There is a tremendous force in the universe that can be tapped into."

I thought about the force and asked once again for protection and additional guidance from the universal spirits. I wouldn't tell Valerie about Holly's warning.

Chapter Twenty-Four

We had a couple, Carol and Daniel, on the phone. This client spoke briefly about Hagerstown, Maryland, and how nice a place it was to live, though the winters were rather rough compared to Florida.

As the husband and wife spoke to me, I visualized several spirits, young, old, infants, all trying to send messages at the same time. I allow this to go on for what seems like forever, but in reality, it lasts only about thirty seconds. Finally, one spirit's force overpowers the others. Other spirits remain, trying to communicate, but the leading spirit drowns them out until they give in. finally, the overpowering spirits were an old couple going by the names Vivian and Harry.

"Carol, I'm getting the names of Vivian and Harry. They appear to be older. Do those names mean anything to you?"

"Yes, they are my parents," Carol responded. "The last name would be Cole. My maiden name was Cole."

"Okay. Yes, they are agreeing. They send you both love and assure you that the family members who have passed are all there together. Harry is showing me a young man, a child, who stays with them. He is watching over him. I'm getting a name here. One second, please. Sounds like Aspero? Osprey? Does this mean anything?"

"My God!" Carol exclaimed. "That is Aspen! That is our son, Aspen!"

"He is safe with Vivian and Harry. He is smiling down at you both. He is telling me, Aspen is, that he watches you both and is with you in your living room every evening while you both watch the telly; Jeopardy, and Wheel of Fortune shows."

"Yes, Marjorie, we watch those shows almost every night. You are saying Aspen is in the room with us?"

"Yes. He is telling me you even cover yourself with a brown crocheted blanket. The one that has yellow and orange in it, but mostly brown. He says you are usually cold while his father is usually warm and runs the air way too much."

"Wow, that is right," she laughed.

"I'm amazed," Marjorie. "Tell our son how much we miss him."

"Oh, he knows that. They know what we are thinking when they are near us."

"Aspen wants you to be assured that he is happy and is surrounded by all loved family members who have passed too. There are great grandfathers and great grandmothers, great cousins, and so many others. He is telling me that please live your life and enjoy your time on Earth. But be assured that death is but a brand-new beginning that should be welcomed. He is telling me to stress that the reward to a life well lived is enjoyed in the afterlife. And you will be greeted personally by Aspen when it is your time to pass."

Our reading went well. Carol and Daniel were also visited by friends and neighbors who had passed. They were surprised when the messages received were right on the money. Spirits know how to bring to light things only people at the reading would recognize and know to be factual.

The first reading was over, and I was a little tired. Valerie and I had some hot tea as we discussed how well the reading went. There are some readings that don't go well. Sometimes spirit gives many dates and names that just don't hit home with the clients we do readings for. Sometimes it may take days or weeks for a person to call me, all excited because the information that didn't make sense during the reading finally makes perfect sense.

"You have been very fortunate for the last several readings, Marjorie. You hit home with the clients. Spirit really clicked with the details," Valerie said.

"Yes, sometimes like a television screen, the picture and messages come in high definition. Then other times, it all seems like it is very blurry. We never know ahead of time what will transpire."

As I was finishing my tea and while Valerie was cleaning up in the kitchen, something strange happened. Suddenly, I had rapid flashes running through my mind. It was so fast that I couldn't make out the face of the man.

Spirits can sometimes play tricks, as they can be playful at times. They don't mean to frighten us, at least many don't, but there are rogue spirits that will want to frighten us for various reasons. But mostly, it is the playful spirits that play tricks, as if it were Halloween all the time.

This was not one of those times. The rapid succession of visuals was so fast and bright that I was beginning to feel dizzy, lightheaded, and I was suddenly perspiring. I felt for one solid minute like I would pass out.

The flashes continued. When I tried to get out of the kitchen chair, the room spun out of control. I felt as if I had the worst drunken hangover ever. I quickly sat down. Valerie noticed me and quickly moved closer.

"Are you all right, Marjorie?" she asked as she put a hand on my shoulder.

"I am just fine!" I lied, not wanting to alarm her. "I just feel a little lightheaded." Meanwhile, the flashes increased in speed, making it hard to think, speak properly, or recognize anyone in particular.

"Let me help you to the recliner. We still have a couple of hours before the next reading."

We made it slowly over to the living room recliner, and I collapsed into the pillowy softness. Quickly, I closed my eyes and told Valerie that I would try to get a quick nap but not to allow me to sleep long. I needed her to back off.

It finally worked. Valerie was busying herself. The flashes in my brain were like a strobe light, relentless in its bright flashes of unintelligible people.

Finally, unexplainably, the strobing slowed, and I caught a quick glimpse of a person who looked familiar. As I tried to place the person, the flashing quickened again relentlessly.

I thought, who was this person that I had only a split-second view of? All of a sudden, it materialized. The vision that had flashed so fast was that of the tire slasher from the mall, Angel Diaz, the skinny guy with the scarred face.

What could this message mean? Was there a problem with this man? Did Carlo DiLingo take care of my problem with him in some violent way? I have heard of problems in the mafia that mysteriously disappear. Am I seeing Angel Diaz's spirit from the beyond?

I felt so bad disclosing any of my problems with Diaz to Carlo. What was I thinking? Carlo DiLingo had a bad reputation. I did Carlo a considerable favor, possibly saving his wife's life. What did I expect Carlo to do? This was the same man who said he would do anything at all for me. He would move Heaven and hell to help me. I should have kept Angel Diaz all to myself.

Just as quickly as the visions strobed, they stopped. I was, eyes closed, visualizing a blank, black, dark screen. And for the first time in my life, I was scared of the blackness of nothing. But I kept my eyes closed, giving the appearance of sleep to Valerie.

With eyes closed, I tried to reach out to Holly, asking for her help and guidance, but to no avail. Holly will not predict the future for me, only try to guide me away from potential danger. I knew this.

Still, I derive a great deal of comfort seeing her in my mind's eye and hearing her voice inside my head. It is a lonely world inside the psychic mind; Holly makes it so much more tolerant.

Chapter Twenty-Five

It was three o'clock, almost time for our second reading. I actually fell off to sleep for a while. Valerie let me sleep, knowing I needed some downtime before the next reading. If I am overtired, the spirits don't communicate so well. Perhaps they know I am not at my best, almost as if interference is running in the back of my mind. The thoughts get all jumbled in my brain.

Valerie knew that there was way too much excitement for me with the Carlo DiLingo visit, with police protection outside, and the nut job that slashes tires. I had to admit it; usually, I looked forward to helping people with my readings, and spirits that need to get their messages passed on. But now I just wanted to run away to an isolated island, somewhere far away. Somewhere that spirit reception can no longer penetrate.

Valerie had Crystal and Gene on the phone line from Woodbridge, New Jersey. As usual, we knew nothing about Crystal and Gene, except that they were from New Jersey and had waited a long time to speak with me. I felt terrible that people who are sometimes so desperate to seek out loved ones who have passed must wait so long to vent or communicate and have their long-awaited questions answered.

Crystal and I spoke about Woodbridge, New Jersey, for a few minutes, of how she longed to move to Florida to ease her brutal winters there up north. She admitted that it was hard to secure a good-paying job in specific fields and that they may have to wait until retirement.

Once again, there was a mob of spirits that were all anxious to have their say. There were infants, teenagers, many older people, and it seemed like onlookers behind them all.

Of course, the strongest vibe or voice gets in first, drowning out others that try but fail to get their messages through. Everyone has a need to communicate. Some pertain significantly to the client at the reading. Some are distant relatives or acquaintances who want to come by and chat, share a memory, or just say, "Hello, I'm fine."

The overpowering spirit that was leading all the others was saying, "Allow me to get through to Crystal. I need to speak to her." He was very persistent, as are some spirits. And no matter what I would do to try to deter him, it wouldn't work. If I closed myself into a closet somewhere, his communication would continue. If Crystal hung up the phone, he would not go away. Rather, he would continue communicating until he got exactly what he wanted across to me, even if he took an extra week to get me to listen and pass along to the intended party.

"Crystal," I began. "I have an elderly gentleman who is very persistent by the name of Thomas. Does the name Thomas ring a bell?"

"Thomas? I don't recollect a Thomas. There are people we know named Thomas at work, at church, even a cousin, but they are all young," she said hesitantly.

"Okay, Thomas is impatiently telling me he is related. He keeps repeating that he is the father of John Sata or Seta. Something like that. Does that help you? He is an excitable kind of guy, very persistent."

"Oh, yes," she said. "John is my grandfather. The last name is *Saista*. So, it is John and Michelle Saista, my grandparents. I believe that Thomas is Michelle's father. So, Thomas is my great-grandfather.

"That is amazing. Thomas is communicating with us now?" Crystal asked.

"Non-stop! He is going so fast that I cannot keep up with him. Thomas admits he is your great-grandfather, and he is there along with your father and mother, and John and Michelle Saista, your grandparents. We are here with Rochelle. She is fine, always with family and friends, and she loves you both very much. Rochelle wants you to move on and live your life to the fullest. She says that she watches over you in your darkest hour. She is there for all the fun times. And Rochelle is protecting you from yourself, your deepest worries, your depression over her death."

"Marjorie, my daughter Rochelle, is she with us now? Is she there? Can she see us now?"

"Rochelle is a young woman who is with Thomas, her great, great-grandfather, and the others. They are all surrounding the lovely blonde woman by the name of Rochelle. Yes, she sees us. Yes, she is sending rays of love out to you both. She wants you to know she is very much at peace now."

"Oh, thank God. We were so worried about our daughter."

"Rochelle wants you to know that she did not suffer in death. Rochelle was at peace when she passed, carried over to the other side by Thomas, her great, great-grandfather."

"Oh, I am so relieved."

"I am receiving thoughts that your daughter was killed. Is this correct? And do you want to discuss this at all, Crystal and Gene?"

I knew this was an excruciating wound that I was slicing open. I knew it would be challenging, even on me, but it was the only way for the ongoing wound to finally begin to heal, instead of being constantly sliced open many times more.

Gene spoke up rather quickly, protecting Crystal from further pain from speaking about the horrific experience and memories.

"Our daughter was on vacation over five years ago with her girlfriends. They were on vacation in Acapulco. It was a bachelorette party for Sandy Crinlon, her best friend, to take place the next day.

"Rochelle had been out drinking with her friends that first night. She met up with a young man named Miguel Torres. They took off to walk on the beach late that night. They never returned—our daughter was found dead, along with Miguel, the next day. They were found floating in the ocean.

"Our daughter's killers were never caught. Both Miguel and Rochelle had had their throats slit…"

I could hear sobbing on the line, and Gene's voice was cracking. There was silence. I allowed it all to sink in and calm down. Then I spoke. "Rochelle is telling me that it was drug-related, the deaths of Miguel and her…"

"Our daughter did not do drugs. Never, ever, did she do any drugs!" Crystal blurted out.

"Let's take a minute here, please," I said. "We need to clarify any messages I am receiving."

There was silence for what seemed to be hours. But in reality, it might have been thirty very long seconds.

"Crystal and Gene, Rochelle is telling me that she did not do drugs on a regular basis, though she had experimented with some a couple of times. Miguel and she were in fact killed over drugs, though."

Gene spoke up again, "Does Rochelle tell you who was the person who murdered her?"

"All she is saying is this: a powerful drug cartel was responsible for their murders. Miguel, unknown to Rochelle, was involved in the drug trade. It appears that Miguel stole a large amount of money and drugs from the powerful cartel. He and your daughter were killed in retaliation for the grave mistake Miguel made.

"No one has been brought to justice, and no one will in the future. The cartel is just too powerful in Mexico, much too powerful for the authorities. The authorities are being bribed, in many instances, to look the other way. This is how this particular cartel has thrived in Mexico to be the most powerful drug cartel in the world. So, Rochelle is stressing that you must both move on and give up the false hope that justice will be done."

I had tears in my eyes as I passed on Rochelle's communications to me. The visions the parents saw from the words I passed on from Rochelle were enough to send a dagger into their hearts. But I was sure in the end it was something they secretly had been praying for more than five years. The only way to receive some form of closure was to hear the reality of the end of their daughter's life. And have the assurance that Rochelle was at peace for eternity.

Crystal spoke through her sobbing, "Marjorie, we had a great suspicion in Miguel. We were certain that he personally did no harm to our daughter, but we suspected his involvement in some sort of illegal activity. Rochelle was a good girl. Maybe that was her downfall—too trusting, too loving, too innocent for a world full of temptations and lots of evil."

"Yes," Gene said. "Marjorie, we thank you from the bottom of our hearts for reminding us that a soul goes on for eternity. And although a person passes on, it does not mean that their involvement in your life ends. We needed this so bad. We needed that jolt to know for sure that Rochelle is still with us and that we will be reunited with her one day for certain."

It never gets old; the inner sense of worth I feel when people I do readings for acknowledging and embracing the spirit of a departed loved one. When they finally start to look forward, as spirit begs them, to living the rest of their lives and enjoying the rest of their lives. Many people stay in a pit of self-imposed poison when the love of their lives is savagely and abruptly ripped away from them forever. It warms my heart to improve upon that.

Chapter Twenty-Six

After the reading for Crystal and Gene was over, I was downright tuckered out. More than I could remember in recent months. Valerie was concerned once again that I was overdoing the readings. It was five o'clock, and she insisted that I take a nap for a half-hour. There was no fighting her on the matter, as she said, "I will personally knock you out myself if you don't go and lie down right now."

It didn't take too much convincing, as I was feeling weak, and my eyes were closing on their own. I knew I was drained. The schedule had been grueling for the past few months, and it was finally taking a toll on me.

With my eyes closed, resting in my bed, I reviewed the death of Rochelle and Miguel. And I tried to visualize how brutal the end of their lives was. With the visions of their throats cut, I slowly fell off to sleep. I saw Rochelle smiling approvingly at me, and the vision went dark.

Dreams come and go about random weird things. Sometimes unexplainable things present themselves as dreams. Some we remember, many we routinely forget, but all of them we are one hundred percent certain are dreams and not real. Then there are those intense visions that are messages from the beyond. Those particular messages differ significantly from dreams. Our souls are interacting in real-time with spirits that, for whatever reasons, choose to do so while we are fast asleep.

I knew full well that the visions I was seeing were definitely not dreams. They were messages from beyond. They were communications with my soul, which was out there in the unknown, needing to receive visions and communications. The movie-like thoughts played out in high definition. First, there was a community, a silent community, almost identical to a movie set. There was virtually no activity, eerie-like in a way.

The voice I was hearing told me that it was where he lived while alive—a retirement community for over age fifty-five people. The state was New Hampshire. I could see large mounds of pure white snow. The homes were very similar in style, condition, colors, and were new in appearance.

His name was Sidney. He told me he was gay while alive, that for most of his life, he was picked on, discriminated against, and bullied as a child. Kids routinely beat Sidney up. Sidney disclosed to me that he was murdered.

I asked him, "Why?"

"I was considered a newbie. I was different, and I didn't fit in with many of the older residents."

"But you were not the only new gay man the community had ever encountered, were you?"

"No, but I wanted to run for president of the building's coalition committee. There were older residents that didn't want me. I had many new ideas. I wanted to make many changes, raise the dues, hire security around the clock, and change the allowable colors and structure construction choices for residents looking to modify their homes. Some people were very much against this."

"Do they know who killed you?"

"They have no clue. The police have an ongoing investigation, but there are no suspects. You see, Marjorie, I was adopted from Israel as a young infant by a couple who could not bear children. I was an only child. When I passed away, I was 66, never married, had no children, and was a retired CPA."

"Do you have any surviving family, Sidney?"

"That is just it. You see, right before I died, I had connected, through DNA tests, with twin biological sisters who also were adopted by a family and are living in New York. They are close. They were adopted together by a lawyer and his wife in Manhattan. They are older, age 70. Our biological parents and all the adoptive parents have all passed. We had just found each other six months before I was killed. They need to know who did this…"

"All they know now is that you were killed?"

"Yes, I was found at the bottom of the lake at the community. Paving stones were tied to my body to keep it at the bottom. You have to let the authorities and my sisters know who did this. This person is dangerous."

"Do you know what happened to you, Sidney?"

"I was poisoned, Marjorie. I was sent a batch of cookies for my birthday. They were a mixed batch of homemade cookies. The gift card sent with the package said they were sent from our community association. Of course, that was not true.

"There had been many rumors of someone cutting lanai screens, breaking windows, cutting people's electric lines, but never, to my knowledge, killing people."

"Did anyone suspect someone doing these things, Sidney?"

"Well, yes. They believed that it was someone who despised the newer people moving into the community. Our community has over two thousand homes. The community is twenty years old and almost all built up. There are so many newcomers and still some who have been there since the first home was built.

"There is a man who is as mean as a rattlesnake. He was there when the first homes were built. It is said that he had a large dog for 12 years, a German shepherd. The dog and his wife both died five years ago. He is around eighty-five and is going senile. He hates everyone. He yells at all the landscapers, plumbers, and all other contractors still building in the community.

"He complains about everyone and anything that is close to him or annoys him in any way. Everyone knows him to be a bitter individual."

"So, how did he dispose of you, so to speak? He is old?"

"Simple. I'm located in the lake. The rear of my home faced the lake, only fifteen feet behind the lanai. What he did was break into the lanai once he knew I was poisoned from the cookies. We all keep our patio doors open on the lanai to catch the crosswinds on a hot night.

"Around midnight, the old man, I'm told by my loving spirit relatives, broke the tiny lock on the lanai screen door. He came into my house and wheeled my dead body to the lake behind the house with a hand truck. He took my body by rowboat to the center of the lake. He weighed me down with paving stones he had taken from a home under construction and pushed my body overboard."

"So, no one could figure out what he had done?"

"Suspicion is one thing; the proof is another. People always look to him whenever anything goes wrong in the community, but there was nothing that showed he was the murderer. In fact, he purposely broke the security gate to the community by tying it in the open position after breaking the camera from behind."

"He, no doubt, planned this act for some time, didn't he?" I said.

"Brilliant plan," Sidney added.

"What proof ties him to the crime? A jury will never convict someone without indisputable proof."

"Yes, I agree," he said. "We have such proof. He used his dead German shepherd's metal chain to tie the pavers to my belt. It has the dog's name, Ronnie, on it, along with a phone number, Sidney's cell phone number. Also, the boat he used that night was his own. My DNA is in that boat, according to my relative spirits."

"That is what we needed, Sidney. I can now pass this on to my FBI contact, Carl Higgins. He will look into the ongoing investigation and contact your sisters in New York."

"There is one other thing, Marjorie. Please take extra care of your safety. I am feeling much tension concerning your safety. Don't take any foolish chances with your actions."

"Do you see anything specific?" I asked.

"No, just that your recent dealings carry with it much tension in people's minds."

Again, Sidney was over the top in thanking me for helping to solve his murder and ease his sisters' minds. But once again, I was nervous about warnings of possible danger in my life. I was not used to worrying. At no other time did spirits ever tell me to be very careful and that they see much tension inside people's minds. It all started with the spirit's message I received from Julie Flanks, about the double murder in the bar she co-owned. This all opened a Pandora's box, revolving around Mafia people and the head of the Litilio Mafia family, Carlo DiLingo.

Why me? Why now? Wasn't there any other psychic out in the universe that they could have picked on? If only I could pick and choose which spirits and messages from the beyond, I could turn off and which to allow into my mind.

For the first time in my life, my eye was twitching. It was my frazzled nerves; I knew that. But there was no turning it off. Isn't it amazing how the mind can set off the body in many strange reactions? Time always seems to solve all the tough times in one's life, so I knew time would get me back to my calmer, laid-back life I so enjoyed.

Chapter Twenty-Seven

It was ten o'clock at night. I was tuckered out from the three sessions I had had that day: the two readings and the impromptu spirit command performance from Sidney, who refused to be turned away. He made sure he pushed me to listen to his urgent need to right a wrong and bring justice to his killer.

I had previously met officer Kent Logan, Jack Krauss's replacement for the week. Kent was wonderful and outgoing as he knocked on the door and introduced himself. Kent was young, around 24, tall, slim, and had brown hair and eyes. We had a couple of cookies together as he explained that he was on the force for one year.

Kent told me that the first year as an officer was the hardest. That citizens don't give respect that the older officers receive. People gave him a harder time when he made a legal stop of someone. He had to go way overboard with patience and kindness to everyone, even other officers in his own station house, who hadn't yet accepted him fully.

"Are you married, Kent?"

"No, not even close yet. I still live home with my parents. I am still paying back huge college loans. So, it may be awhile before I can think of getting hitched."

He had a boyish smile and charm to him as we said goodnight, and he retreated to his cruiser for the night. I felt so much better after meeting Kent, knowing he would go above and beyond to protect me.

I tried to watch television, the History Channel, some nature program. The wilderness was beautiful, and the music was relaxing. My eyes wouldn't stay open. As I slept, my mind wandered to snow. I was dreaming because it was snowing heavily right outside my window. In my dream, I grabbed a camera and started to take pictures. The trees were full of snow, and the branches were glistening white and heavy. But it is Florida; it is not supposed to snow in Florida, no less in Fort Lauderdale, Florida, so far south.

There is no control over dreams. They come in rapid succession at times, changing to various storylines and locations along the way.

Suddenly, my dream changed to the wilderness, and there were wild boars that were chasing me. I was screaming at no one who could hear me. The boars were in a group and catching up to me. All of a sudden, I slipped, and the boars all jumped on me, biting and scratching. I knew I would die, and there was nothing I could do about it. I was never so scared in my life. Just before I thought I would die, I woke up, jumping up from the sofa.

It was a few seconds before I realized what had happened. I hate those kinds of dreams that scare one to wits' end. Why those kinds of dreams happen, I will never know. Perhaps it is from simmering thoughts deep in our subconscious mind? They reproduce themselves in a variety of sorts in our dreams.

I sat back down, looking at birds flying high in the bluest of skies on the television show. I was just staring at the screen, almost mesmerized, yawning and tired, and wondering about life. What was it all about, this life on Earth? If it is to be so short, then why do we live it on Earth at all? Why not just be in the hereafter right from the beginning of life?

Why do we need to see all the joys on Earth, all the wondrous times, only to be exposed to all the heartache we all encounter at various times throughout our short span of time on Earth? We see our loved ones suffer, get sick, then die, sometimes with a great deal of pain and suffering. We then lose them, only to suffer ourselves greatly, wondering, *Why them? Why not me?* But yet, we are the ones now in pain mentally, not physically. Time does heal our mindful hurt, only to be hurt again. *So, what is it all about*, I wondered?

At that precise moment, I heard a voice and saw many spirits. They were all dressed in white, of all ages, all sizes and shapes, and nationalities. But only one elderly man with a long white beard spoke.

"My dear Marjorie, life on Earth is but a valuable lesson that must be experienced, must be savored, must be learned from. As a child plays a sports game, each time they play, they are trying to improve, are they not? The improvement is an internal need to learn, to better themselves, to excel. Though it may not happen for many times played, sooner or later they will be better, they will learn, they will feel victorious, not for others, not for winning, but rather for improving, even ever so slightly over what they were.

"Such is life. An improvement over prior days, years, minutes, and even improvements over previous hereditary lives of past family members long ago passed on.

"You are correct; life on Earth is but minute specks of time until eternity is presented to that life form. Eternity is everything. So, you wonder, why even bother with experiences on Earth? An infant, from the moment they open their eyes, is always learning, improving, reinventing themselves. They study others, emulate others and always try to improve over what they observe from others.

"You speak of joy, of pain, of despair, and of hurt from the loss of loved ones. You wonder why. What is the purpose of the pain of watching other loved ones in pain, slowly dying, and finally passing on? It is a lesson of life. If not the pain, if not the love of another, if not the hurt of the loss of a loved one, then what would the value of life be to anyone?

"The priceless life of an individual comes only from the witnessing of pain, death, suffering, love of those they are surrounded by in their own life. After one passes from their temporary earthly time given, and continues their journey for an eternity, they take with them those valuable lessons of love, suffering, pain, hurt, and of dying. They have been trained, no matter how long they lived on Earth. Only then can they truly experience the eternal wonders of the hereafter, which will extend the learning a billion times more in-depth."

"So, we are to improve as far as we can while on Earth? That is of utmost importance?"

"With a love for everything and everyone, yes. One is to improve to the utmost of their ability. For that is all a person who passes will carry forward for eternity. Did they pass, in their own evaluation, with their life on Earth, or merely waste the miracle gift of life they were blessed with?"

Suddenly, the vision went away. The voices all stopped, and the television took over in image and sound, leaving me to contemplate what spirit taught me about life and death.

Who was the older man? Who were all the others, also dressed in all white? Were all these people the most intelligent beings that once graced the Earth? Were they there to educate? Are these the ones that greet those who pass on to the hereafter?

After a hot tea with honey and a couple of Lorna Doone cookies, I fell off to a sound sleep. It is incredible that when awakened, you believe you were sound asleep for hours when sometimes it is merely minutes. My sound sleep lasted ten minutes as I woke up to the sounds of someone in the back of the house.

At first, I thought it could be a dog or cat scratching on the back walls of the house. Kent was right out in front. But the noise was louder, and I soon became frightened. The louder it became, the more I realized that someone was jimmying the glass patio doors of the house.

I was too scared to move, too afraid to yell out if anyone was there, and too frightened to scream. The closest phone was in the kitchen, a wall phone, and my cell phone was lying on the kitchen counter. The patio was right at the rear of the kitchen, so I dared not make a dash to the kitchen. But what do I do?

I didn't want to run out the front door, out into the dark of night, totally exposed to whatever danger could be present. I couldn't call Valerie. I couldn't call the police, and I couldn't run out of the house.

Chapter Twenty-Eight

The sound of the metal pressing hard against metal filled the air. Someone was intent on breaking through the locked aluminum sliding glass patio doors. I knew I had to run, but where could I be safe? The bedrooms had no lock on their entrance doors, and there were windows in each of the two bedrooms. That didn't appear safe to me.

Then there was a basement, also with no locking mechanism on the door. I would be a sitting duck in the basement, so that option was out of the question. There was the attic option. There was a pull-down stairway that led up to the attic. But all I could see was someone coming up the attic and trapping me, with no exit.

"So, what now?" I said to no one as the door to the back of the house was being compromised. I could hear that the person was making headway in breaking the lock.

I figured the best defense was an offense. I quickly got up, ran to the basement door, opened it, and put on the light. I then pulled hard on the cord to that hallway attic stairway, pulling the stairway down and flipping on the attic light. Then I ran into the master bedroom, but before I did, I locked and closed the hallway bathroom door, making it appear that I was locked in there.

I retreated to my master bedroom bathroom and locked the door behind me. I stayed as quiet as a church mouse, not even breathing more than what was absolutely necessary for survival. I quickly opened the vanity cabinet drawer and grabbed the emergency cigarette lighter I kept there to light candles in case of a power failure. I figured I could light the cigarette lighter up and keep the lights off. This way, no one could see me.

Before I shut the light off, I got a fabulous idea: Let me arm myself with a weapon. I had no guns like so many people today that arm themselves for the protection of themselves and their families. I didn't believe in guns put into everyone's hands. Most people would never be able to operate a firearm when suddenly faced with a life-or-death situation.

No, I found something even I could handle without killing myself. At least, I hoped I could. I reached into the vanity cabinet and took out a large can of hairspray. I read somewhere that if you light up the spray from a deployed hairspray, it could become like a blowtorch.

This was my only idea. This was my sole line of protection from an armed intruder with trouble on their mind. What else could I do? I had no time to plan, to run, to escape.

I could hear someone in the house moving around. It is incredible that when we strain, in a quiet night, we can distinguish even the slightest sounds rummaging through our house.

Now I wasn't breathing at all as I heard a voice, "Ghost woman, where are you? I know you are home, so come out. I won't harm you because I will kill you. You hurt me bad.

You cut into my heart with Carlo. Because of you, I will be isolated instead of becoming a made man.

"You have to die, so come out. Don't try to scare me with your ghost friends. I have a 38 revolver. I am not scared of ghosts. Are you up there in the attic? Or in the basement? You know you cannot hide from me! The cop is dead. Did you think one cop all by himself could protect you from the mafia, Ghost Lady?

"You have a big mouth! You ruined it all with your big fat mouth. Carlo's brother-in-law will rot in jail because of you. So, you have to die; it's only fair."

I heard the footsteps and creaking on the folding attic stairs. "I know you're up there, you bitch. So just tell me. Don't make it any harder on yourself."

I heard walking in the attic, slowly from one end to the other. Then the steps again.

"Okay, this is going to be fun, like a treasure hunt. I will find you. You cannot hide in this small house."

The voice was getting lower and lower. I was sure that Angel Diaz, the man with the long, scarred face from the mall, was going to kill me. I was nervous that when Carlo got involved in the tire-slashing incident, there would be anger. I had no idea it would come to this.

Spirit tried to warn me, but how does one protect themselves all the time, every minute of every day? I already had armed protection. Then, suddenly, it hit me. What did he do? He killed a police officer, the young Kent Logan, a man whose life was just in the early stages.

I sobbed as softly as I could, tears running down my face as I mourned the young man. Was I scared to die? I think everyone is scared to be killed. We all want it to end when we want and not a moment sooner. But in reality, I had a wonderful life, no regrets. Well, maybe a few.

I always wanted to jump from a plane, in a parachute, of course. I always wanted to own a horse but not clean up the smelly part. I always wanted to eat dinner at the White House and have a current President give me a personal tour. Other than that, I have done it all, had it all, loved it all. If I had to go, I guess I could. I only wished that Kent could live and I would be the only dead one.

After all, it was all anger against me. I was the one who slapped a hornets' nest. Should I have refused to get involved in the double murders of the bar? Perhaps. But then I would have to face a different anger from a different person—me. The quote that comes to mind is, "To thine own self be true." We all make choices in our lives. We can't over-analyze every decision in our lives, or we would wind up in a looney bin.

The footsteps got louder, and his voice was closer now. "You tried to fool me; you did. But you are running out of time now. Do ghosts pray? You better say your prayers now, Ghost Lady!"

He was walking into the spare bedroom. Then he was forcing open the hallway bathroom. He was now walking closer.

"So, you think you are smart! I am getting warm now, ain't I, Ghost Lady?"

He was getting really close. My heart was pounding so hard I could hear it tapping out a drum roll. I held onto the can of hairspray with one hand and the bathroom doorknob with the other.

He was right outside the door now. He had opened the closet doors in the bedroom. He looked under the bed as he said, "I thought you would be under the bed. This was a little fun, Ghost Lady. I may even feel bad after I kill you. But I have to even the score. You understand, I'm sure. We can't let people like you control our destiny. After all, who would then fear the mafia?"

His voice was now on the other side of the bathroom door. I could feel the door now move ever so slightly. The locks are very minimal in bathrooms and no match for maniacs like Angel Diaz. I quickly grabbed the lighter and readied it away from the nozzle of the spray can.

"Do you want to come out and make this easy on yourself? Okay, then I'm coming in."

I heard the jamming of a tool of some kind into the jamb of the door. The door was starting to move away from the jamb as he was pulling on the handle, trying to open it.

I had my weapon ready and was close to lighting the spray can.

Finally, I heard the cracking sound of the lock breaking away from the door jamb, and he started to pull the door to himself. It was time. Do or die. I quickly lit the lighter and pressed the nozzle of the spray can, sending a blast of fire through the slightly open door.

I heard a scream as the fire blasted a part of Angel Diaz's face.

"You son of a bitch! I'm going to torture you now!" he shouted as gunshots rang out. I continued spraying; he continued shooting, now from a distance. The bullets ricocheted through the bathroom.

There were more shots in rapid succession, then a blood-curdling scream. "No, no!" he screamed.

Then I heard a thud and no more shots. Did I burn Angel's eyes? Is he rolling on the floor in pain or just not moving at all? Then, I heard a voice, "Marjorie, it's Jack, Officer Jack Krauss. It's all over now! You are safe. He is dead!"

"Marjorie, can I open the door?" Jack said softly in a non-threatening way. I didn't answer.

"It's over; the man is dead now. There is nothing to worry about now. I am going to slowly open this door now, Marjorie. You are safe now. Okay?"

"Yes," was all I could say. I was numb.

I was wet with what could easily be blood. Slowly, I checked myself. There was a little stream of blood running down my hand. I was now dizzy, passing out, knowing I had been shot.

The last thing I remember was the door opening, seeing Officer Jack Krauss, and passing out. Again, it could have been days that I was unresponsive, but it was a mere ten minutes. I was already on a stretcher. The paramedics already had my arm bandaged, and Officer Jack Krauss was right there for me.

"Marjorie, you are a real warrior! If this were the military, you would have been in line for a Purple Heart. You are fine. You only received a flesh wound in your upper right arm. The bullet grazed your arm. You are very fortunate, young lady. You very easily could be dead, except you fought off that creep."

I could see a blanket-covered body of Angel Diaz. "Is he…"

"Dead as the dirty rotten dog he was. There was no doubt in my mind. He would have never allowed himself to be taken alive. I had to take him out. I am so glad I did."

"But Jack, what about Officer Kent Logan?"

"Kent is alive but in critical condition."

"My God! So, he did shoot Kent!"

"Kent was shot in the back of his head through the rear window of the cruiser. Perhaps a silencer was used. He had no chance to thwart the attack or respond. But God was looking down on Kent. Because the bullet, though entering at the base of the skull, ricocheted and exited just above the ear. Though he is in critical condition, Kent has a good chance at a full recovery. We will know much more in a day or two. We are all praying for him, and half the force is standing guard in the hospital for him."

"Jack, you were supposed to be on vacation!"

"I am. I am taking day trips and staying close to our home, doing chores I never get around to."

"But how did you ever find your way here tonight?"

"I don't really know why. I can't fully explain it, but I heard a female voice that said, 'Check on her.' It sort of freaked me out. But I was concerned about you and concerned for Kent, being that he is still new to the force. I was just going to stop by and chat with Kent for a while. I wasn't going to bother you and perhaps frighten you for no good reason.

"When I pulled up to your property, I quickly sensed something was wrong. I saw the bullet-ridden rear windshield of the cruiser. I quickly entered the house through the back and followed the voice of the intruder. As soon as I saw the shot-up cruiser, I knew you were going to be killed.

"Honestly, I thought I was way too late for you. I felt terrible, like I let you down, even though I had a replacement. That would have been me tonight. And I may not have had the fortune that Kent had. In fact, I have routinely been unlucky in many things so far on Earth."

"Nonsense! You were fortunate in listening to your intuition tonight. You knew enough to physically come over here and check up on Kent and me. You are a great person with a huge heart and a dedication to serving the people, as I have never seen before. So, in reality, you are the luckiest person on Earth, that is, after me, Jack."

I always hated hospitals, and this was no exception. They wheeled me in through the emergency entrance ambulances use. My memories of hospitals were terrible, my husband's last days before dying, friends dying or sick, and tons of spirits hovering around like annoying gnats on a hot, humid night.

Spirits are always visiting the last places they occupied on Earth. They are drawn to the hospital, and if I am there by some chance, they want to share their stories with me. But there are literally thousands, all drowning each other out.

I can't get into it with them, especially at times of emergencies, so I ignore most of it until I can leave.

I was there, according to the paramedics, as a precaution. They needed to monitor me for the night. I needed a tetanus shot for the wound. I needed to replace the bandage and treat the wound with antibiotics. Jack had to leave me after I was admitted and completed a ton of reports about the shootings.

I had three additional police officers guarding my room inside and outside and at the entrance of the hospital. The police chief would take no chances after the latest events.

Who communicated with Jack that night, telling him to check up on Kent and me? Was it Holly? After all, she was my spirit guide. It would make perfect sense for her to continue looking after me as she has for my whole existence.

One never knows when their life will end. I have learned that spirits cannot perform miracles; instead, they must allow many things to play out. Why me? Why was I spared when others perish? I don't know. In fact, I don't really know much except what spirit shares with me. The afterlife is definitely the reward. But we are not supposed to understand it all, or even a minute portion of it, for practical reasons. Would many people, if they knew the potential "Paradise" of the afterlife, opt-out of Earth for the afterlife if convinced it is so much greater than our temporary housing here?

Valerie was at the hospital that next morning, along with Officer Jack, who wanted to bring me home once released. Valerie was in total shock and disbelief about the shooting of the officer and myself, and how I could have died that night.

"I can't believe that I almost lost you for good. How are you dealing with it, Marjorie?"

"I am doing fine, especially since they gave me a few happy pills, which make me a little giddy, dear. I get to take some of these happy pills when I go home, too."

"I could use some of those myself, I tell you!"

"Well, you have to get shot first, Valerie!"

"No, thank you. But I do feel very sad, just the same, about the officer and you. What kind of world do we live in? It's insane at times?"

"We live in a disposable world where wiping out a person or group of people doesn't bother some people any longer. A place where people do evil acts and are unconcerned about ramifications here or in the hereafter; some people today have no fear of facing God. It is a very different world today, my dear. Values have all drastically changed. Life means very little to so many people. Still, the good outnumber the evil, and the strong will always survive over the weak."

"You know that your doctor wants you to take a few days off?"

"Why? I feel wonderful!"

"Maybe a little too wonderful, with those happy pills you seem to like so much."

"Our appointments?"

"All rescheduled."

"No, they waited so long."

"And they will wait for you again. You are very much in demand. And now that you've been featured on the news…"

"No way!"

"Very much, way, yes! That's all there is all over the news. Cop shot, psychic shot, and police officer comes to save the day, killing a Mafia bad man."

"Wow, the more I want to keep a low profile lately, the more publicity I am getting."

"It's great for business. We are booked solid, and the answering machine is now full. I'll get to it later. Meanwhile, we take it easy for a few days and I help you at home."

"I don't need any…"

"You are stuck with me, lady. We can reminisce. We can eat ice cream. And we can watch some old-time movies. We have been working way too hard. Life is too short to kill ourselves. If we die, the world continues to turn; people forget who we are in a matter of days."

"I agree, Valerie. I came very close, once again, to dying. I am starting to wonder that God doesn't want me."

"Be glad!"

"I am not scared of dying, Valerie. Death is the beginning of a great new book and carries with it an unlimited library of knowledge and experiences we cannot even comprehend."

"Yes, I know. Still, I'll stay here, thank you. Maybe they don't allow fattening rocky-road ice cream there? I'll stuff my face here, thank you very much," she laughed loudly.

Jack took me home in a police cruiser, the very first ride I had in a police vehicle. First time for everything, I guess. I was just glad I rode in the front, rather than the back where the criminals all ride.

Valerie and I chilled out. And, as promised, she purchased rocky-road ice cream and made a party of it. I showed her the bullet holes in and out of the master bathroom and the door he destroyed. She understood after I explained what had transpired that Angel Diaz was going to kill me. But he wasn't only going to take my life. He would prolong the agony, make me suffer big for my life, then slowly kill me.

"What a way to die," she said. "He was a sadistic, vengeful creep. No one will miss an animal like that. It played out like a horror movie. I don't know how you didn't crack up," she said.

"I am living on these happy pills they gave me in the hospital," I said as we indulged in huge bowls of ice cream. It really does help, the ice cream binging at times of stress. Thank God we aren't stressed to the extreme every day; otherwise, we'd all be six hundred pounds.

Officer Jack was still on vacation, but promised to return at night to check up on me. I told him, "You better be here, laddie, because I am baking fresh homemade cookies for you and me. By eleven p.m. I will have eaten them all if you haven't shown up."

He responded, "Just don't use that hairspray flame thrower you are famous for. We may add you to our SWAT team!"

The evening was uneventful. There now were two police cruisers outside the house. The police chief wasn't taking any chances, even though Diaz was no longer a threat.

Valerie insisted on sleeping over, and I couldn't convince her otherwise. In fact, I was quite pleased to have her with me. And although there now was double the protection, I couldn't close my eyes in bed. The best I was able to do was tiny naps on the sofa, where I would, out of exhaustion, nod off while Valerie was talking. She understood, and she nodded off, too. At least that was what she admitted to.

All of our appointments were pushed back. Valerie answered all the phone messages, begging off any commitments until further notice. All the callers were very understanding and pleaded for an appointment at all. Many wanted a reading from the "Hairspray Lady," as I was being referred to in the media. There were newspaper stories, television news shows, and even requests for TV and radio interviews of how I fought off the mafia with a spray can.

By five a.m. the next morning, I was cooking a great big breakfast for only the two of us. It was my way of busying my mind, I guessed. But why did I cook waffles, bacon, pancakes, and eggs? There was enough for an army, and I really wasn't hungry. We both picked at everything and had a good laugh about the whole thing.

Valerie and I watched more telly, cartoons of Tom and Jerry, Mickey Mouse, and Popeye. Anything to keep laughing. The police commissioner called to see how I was doing. He also gave me the first updated report on Officer Kent Logan. He said he was in stable condition, improved from critical., he would have no long-term effects from the gunshot wound but would need weeks of recovery. We both said a prayer together, thanking God for His good graces. The commissioner also told me that no other threats existed from the Litilio Mafia family toward me or anyone else in Florida and that this was a random act, not condoned by the mafia in any way.

It was ten o'clock that morning when my FBI friend, Carl Higgins, called me.

"Marjorie, I thank God that you are all right! How is the arm?"

"It was only a flesh wound, Carl. I am fine. The hospital was great. They are sending a nurse, Peggy Hopkins, by eleven o'clock this morning to apply more antibiotic cream and new bandages. It could have been deadly if it hit the artery, but I guess I am blessed."

"Do you know how many prayers are said for you, between all the spirits, the clients you do readings for, and people like me?"

"It's funny you say that, Carl. When I passed out, right after the shooting was over, I heard a distinct voice saying, 'You were put there for a reason, Marjorie Chapman.' It dawned on me when I first came to that; indeed, I was put here for a reason, and I should never belittle that fact."

"I agree, Marjorie; the world needs you and your talent. You are very special. I am so sorry I wasn't there to protect you myself. I feel somewhat responsible."

"Don't talk like that. This would have happened if we had five guards. This man was deranged, intent on revenge. Nothing can counter the intense need for revenge. Anyway, God was also intent to change the inevitable outcome and work a miracle. And it truly was a miracle."

"I agree. We always second guess the events after the fact. Anyway, it worked out. On another note, Carlo DiLingo will be coming to your home at five today…"

"What?"

"Yes, you heard me correctly. I will be there also at five."

"But why? What is the purpose of this Mafia head to come here? His mob associate was just killed in my hallway. What could he possibly want at this point? Is there revenge also on his mind?"

"Please trust me as before, Marjorie. Carlo and any associates he will be with will be disarmed immediately. I had a long discussion with DiLingo. He wants to apologize for the insane actions of Angel Diaz. He assured me that he had no knowledge of Diaz's intent."

"So, he could just call me."

"DiLingo has disclosed to me that he would like to discuss his wife's health update and also make a special announcement while at your home."

"I don't fully understand, Carl. But if you assure me that we all will be safe and that we must accept his visit, I will allow it. I just am not up to seeing him in light of what has transpired."

"You will ultimately be most pleased after speaking with Mr. DiLingo. You know that I am not a huge fan of the Litilio family. And my goal is to squash all illegal activities condoned by the mob. But, DiLingo is trying to change that image, and this visit is a step in that direction."

"I guess I will see you later, Carl?"

"That you will, or maybe you already knew that and you were just teasing me?"

"I am not that good. If I were, I would be sitting at the horse track, waiting for a winner to come to mind."

Chapter Twenty-Nine

We were getting the house ready for the mafia kingpin, Carlo, DiLingo. Valerie was cleaning as if the Queen of England were coming to my home. The person I was looking forward to seeing shortly was the nurse from the hospital, Peggy Hopkins.

When the nurse came, I felt better because I was concerned about infection from the bullet that severed my skin. Peggy Hopkins was a jolly woman with a great sense of humor. "I heard you were auditioning for Wonder Woman, Marjorie. You may be too old for that role?"

"I feel too old for myself, Peggy."

She checked me over very carefully: blood pressure, temperature, pulse, and the gunshot wound. I felt it a little comical that my nurse was short, very round, and overweight. These are the same people that try to tell us how to care for ourselves. I felt that I should be taking her pulse and blood pressure.

She was light-skinned and redheaded. A great lass that I could easily get close to. The wound was cleaned once again, treated with special antibiotic cream, and bandaged again. All the while she was there, I felt a very strong spirit force that wouldn't get weaker. There are times that spirits drop by, look around, maybe observe different people, but then disappear. This spirit force would only get stronger. I knew it was someone very close to Peggy.

Sometimes I am leery about disclosing spirit forms to certain people for concern that they might not receive the message properly or be receptive. Not with Peggy. I was pretty comfortable with her. I waited for the opportune time to disclose the female spirit I had been communicating with to Peggy.

"Peggy, I don't know if you are aware that I am a medium."

"You appear small size to me!" she laughed.

"Funny! I like that one."

"Yes, I read all about you. I must warn you that I am not a big believer in that kind of stuff."

"Not a worry. Most people don't actually know what to expect, but we win them over sooner or later."

"Don't count on me, Marjorie, no offense."

"Well, Peggy, ever since you walked into the house, there has been a persistent entity that has been in the room."

"Really?"

"Yes, a young woman who says her name is Emily. Does that ring a bell, Peggy?"

"Yes, it does," she hesitantly shook her head.

"Is Emily your daughter?" I'm getting that from her.

"Why yes, she was. She passed."

"I'm getting a female-related disease?"

"Yes, that is correct," she said as tears filled her eyes.

"Emily is speaking of a child, the 'S' sound, 'anta'? Something with an 'S.' A young girl you are raising?"

"Okay, now, this is a little weird. Yes, a grandchild named Samantha. Is my daughter really telling you all of this from somewhere?"

"Absolutely! Now, Peggy, it doesn't always work out this good. But in Emily's situation, she is very emotionally drawn to you. She needs to communicate with you. When spirit is that adamant about getting their message received, they will not stop until I convey all their messages.

"Now Emily is speaking about Tommy and a train. I'm sorry, but I can't really make it all out. Is there a connection somehow?"

"Why, yes, there is. I read a book to Emily named 'Tommy, the Little Train.' That is absolutely amazing, Marjorie. I'm sorry for doubting you. I read that you were gifted. They are right."

"Thank you, but Emily is making it quite easy for me. Now she is showing me the turning of a page and a puzzled look on your face."

"Oh, my God, yes. When I put the book down, open-faced, and tend to Samantha for a minute, the page always turns to a different page. It's weird."

"That is Emily, Peggy. That is her way of showing you that she is there with Samantha and you. She is telling me that she is always there when you are reading to her young daughter, and she reads along, too."

"I knew something was up. At first, I thought I had lost my mind. Samantha is only three and a half. Emily passed on when Samantha was only two," she said as she used tissues to wipe her tears.

"I am raising Samantha. Her father only visits once a week. He and Emily divorced six months before she died.

He is a good father, but he is too young to raise Samantha by himself."

"Emily wants you to know that she is with you, your husband, and Samantha very often. She sends messages of love to you all regularly."

Peggy was astounded by the spirit visitation from her daughter. She begged me to do a formal reading for her husband, Samantha, and her. I told her it might be a long wait, but I promised her that we would squeeze her in when we receive a cancellation in the future sometime.

Meanwhile, Peggy made arrangements to come by routinely for dressing and bandage changes. On the way out to her car, she kept shaking her head in disbelief and stopping by one of the police cars to share her story.

It always feels good to lift another person up. I guess the "You are here for a reason" message I received while passed out after the shooting is accurate. We all are here for a reason. Many don't honestly believe that statement, though they verbally may agree with it.

If you don't feel, every day, that there is an important reason you are here, then you may not be able to excel in that search for your personal purpose on this great planet of ours. And what if, by some misguided reason of complacency, you miss the real sense of achievement for yourself? Do we sit somewhere in the hereafter feeling sorry? Do we ponder for eternity that we did not achieve what was the ultimate reason for our existence? How sad. How eternally sad that would be.

Valerie was nervous about a second visit from Carlo DiLingo. She said if it weren't for her love for me, she would run and hide. I told her that I could manage without her, but she wouldn't hear of it.

"I still don't understand why this Mafia big cheese can't just pick up the phone and talk to you! Why does he find it necessary to fly in a private jet from Vegas to Florida just to say something?"

"I am not sure myself, but the man is either looney or has important things he wishes to share with me."

"But it seems trouble follows him wherever he goes and somehow sticks itself right to you."

"I feel like you, Valerie. None of this here mess of things would have taken place if I had not passed on the bar murders from Julie. So, you feel that I should have kept the killer's identity of those two young women to myself, do you?"

"Well, now, I don't really know about that one. I guess I might have done what you have done. But look at what it brought to you."

"Life works in mysterious ways, Valerie. I have learned at least that from all those spirit entities I have communicated with over all the years. It seems like each action has a distinct reaction, though good or bad. There must be a purpose too for what happened. Not all things that happen, though at the outset are horrific, remain horrific. There may be tremendous positive outcomes derived from the terrible onset.

"Look at Carlo's wife, for example. If not for Julie and Crystal coming to me in spirit communication, I would never have received communication from a spirit entity regarding Carlo's wife's undetected cancer. She may live, though others have died. Perhaps it all was supposed to play out that way. You know, we only play a game of life here on Earth, Valerie. We didn't invent the game of life; we don't even understand many of the rules. Yet, we get to play the game the best way we each know and hope we are doing it correctly.

"It is funny in a way, but not until we each pass on to the forever do we get to review all the rules. Only then do we get to see all the answers to the test of life. Only then do we get to say, 'Oh really, now, you couldn't have told me some of those things while I was struggling on Earth?'

"Life is like a Rubik's cube, complicated. You twist it, turn it, want to throw it, and after many attempts, you still don't get it, while some seem to get it in a few seconds. So, welcome to life, Valerie. Just grab your Rubik's cube and twist away."

Chapter Thirty

Carl Higgins was at my home at 4:30 that afternoon. He was discussing the meeting with Litilio family head Carlo DiLingo with the police in front of the house. We now had four police cars outside and five police, one being a Sergeant.

The security was heavy, as it was after the shooting, and I had been in the hospital. My home was closed down for the police investigation for at least twelve hours that day. Carl told me that the reason for the five officers and his two additional FBI agents was not just for my protection. There had been rumors out in law enforcement that someone may want to take over the reins from Litilio family mob head, DiLingo.

"As a precaution," Carl said, "we have to take all rumors seriously. Carlo, we are sure, knows more about these rumors than we do, but it runs in his line of work."

As I was speaking with Carl, I was surrounded by spirit entities, which is not unusual in settings where there are many people; but there shouldn't have been that many spirits for that number of people at that time.

"Do you feel nervous seeing Carlo again after the attack from Diaz?" Carl asked.

"Not really, Carl. For some strange reason, I am more at peace today than I have been. You know, people don't want to hear this from me, but I am not afraid of dying any longer. Does that sound foolish?"

"Actually, if anyone would not be frightened of death and the unknown, it would be you. For so many years, you have been communicating with countless spirits from all backgrounds and with all different messages. The afterlife should be less mysterious, confusing, and worrisome for you than for others."

"I guess you are right. And sometimes, I feel it would be very selfish on my part even to want to pass over to the other side. But it is just how I feel. On the other hand, the hereafter has sent me a message that I still have essential and much-needed work here on Earth. So, I am here as long as God wants me to remain."

"Lucky for us," Carl smiled as he hugged me. "Still no winning lottery numbers I could play?"

"Not a chance. You wouldn't want the money that way, anyway, would you?"

"I could force myself to accept that kind of money, trust me."

We laughed and thought of ways he would spend his windfall if he won. He wanted horses.

"We have all the roads blocked off with officers as a precaution, Marjorie. All drivers will be stopped and checked out, and of course, only authorized people will be allowed access to the vicinity."

I felt very safe, as if the Pope were paying a visit. Valerie was more nervous. Her face was flushed, and I was convinced that her blood pressure was elevated.

"Calm down, girl. I was the one who was shot."

"I know. I think I am more worried about you. After all, you are more of a threat to Carlo, 'Big Hands' than I am. You could have them all locked up if the right spirits start spilling their guts."

"Never really thought of it in that way. Maybe I should be more frightened?"

"No, I guess not. There are so many loaded guns out there. We should be fine. Just don't come up with any Earth-shattering messages from spirits with a vendetta against the main mafia man, Carlo, okay?"

At five-twenty, the entourage arrived, large white SUVs numbering four. I believed that Carlo was being extra careful and had bodyguards this time.

Valerie had been busy in the kitchen preparing Italian hero sandwiches and cold salads. It was going to be like a picnic inside my home. We had gathered a lot of food, just to be on the safe side. I only hoped that they would at least hang around to eat. Then I would be delighted to see them all leave and never return again. I never intended to become chummy with members of a Mafia family. It would be good to go back to dull again. Boring sometimes can be therapeutic and beneficial in extending one's life.

Carl was outside, along with the police gang. They were making sure that no weapons remained with any of the non-security associates of DiLingo. I didn't want to watch any of it. I was, in fact, trying to sort through the many spirit entities that were crowding around in my mind, trying to get top rating for exclusive communication with me.

I was very curious about receiving an update from Carlo regarding his wife, Angelina's, cancer diagnosis. Spirit doesn't give updates; they only pass on troubling potential problems, making sure the person takes symptoms they may not be fully aware of seriously. In the end, neither I nor the forces of the spirits can save everyone. I only do what I have to so people are aware of possible problems.

It was Gus Fauci, the tall attorney for Carlo, who entered the house first. He was very happy to see me. He hugged me quickly, then made room for Carlo to enter.

At six foot three and two hundred seventy pounds, Carlo was like a huge bear as he bent down, hugged me long and firm, and kissed me on each cheek. I felt a little awkward knowing he was the head of the Litilio Mafia family. I try to act like I am not intimidated by the mafia in my home, but it scared the 'willies' right out of me.

"My dear, Marjorie, I am so happy we could meet again in person. I am devastated about the insane behavior of that asshole, Diaz. He was in no way representing my organization or me. And if I were here, I would have strangled him with my bare hands. You are an extension of Heaven. You are our angel here on Earth. You truly are a magnificent, gifted person."

"Thank you, Carlo. In no way do I hold you responsible for a person who went off the deep end. But I have been very concerned about, and praying for, Angelina."

We all sat down in the living room: Carl, Carlo, Gus and me. Valerie had laid out a platter of heroes and drinks and quickly disappeared into the kitchen.

We each sipped the freshly made iced tea as we spoke.

"Without further ado, Marjorie, let me calm your nerves about Angelina. You, of course, were right. She not only had symptoms that were being overlooked, but she had cancer, just as you had suspected.

"Her thyroid is definitely affected. The specialists are personal friends of mine. They plan to remove the thyroid and treat the surrounding tissue. Angelina's prognosis is excellent, as long as she receives the ongoing special new treatment the doctors are using these days.

"Medical technology, they tell me, is so advanced for cancers of this kind. Of course, Angelina was blown away when the diagnosis was first disclosed. But my doctor friends put her mind at ease. The mere word 'cancer' is enough to give the toughest person a coronary, by God! So, all in all, we are fortunate. God is good to us."

"Thank God, Carlo. I do worry because even though spirit warns of something well in advance, we have no way of knowing how advanced something might be. Life is not guaranteed."

"I agree! I jump on private planes as people walk around the block. Everything has a potential risk to it, including my line of work, too."

"I wouldn't know about that," I said.

"Well, trust me, for more than half of my life, there have been many people who secretly want me dead. I know that. Sometimes I don't fall off to sleep at night. Funny, isn't it? As big a guy as I am, I can't be certain that I will be alive tomorrow."

"I did feel a minute bit of fear, Carlo, when Mr. Diaz was stalking me at the mall and my tire was slashed. I can sort of understand what fear you live with each day. I don't think I could survive living like that every day. I feel sorry for you."

"Thank you, don't. My mother said to me many years ago, 'We all make choices in life. You must live, Carlo, with whatever choices you make in life. Don't ever forget that.' I never did forget that, Marjorie. I live with my choices. That is life. That is the life I chose."

"I do have spirit entities present that are here for you, Carlo. We can discuss…"

"Marjorie, please allow me a few minutes to speak with you first, okay?"

"Of course. The spirits that have something to communicate will wait. Trust me, though, they will not leave. It is amazing; really, spirits are like two-year-old children that want a parent's attention. They will do anything to get the full attention of a parent, or in this case, get the complete attention of the psychic they need to communicate their messages to a client."

"I see. That is very interesting. I am so thankful that Angelina's relative, spirit, was so persistent in getting her message through. They saved my wife's life."

"Yes. That is why we never ignore messages that are so urgent and important to spirit entities. They wouldn't go away anyway if they had something so earth-shattering in importance to them. Thank God, most spirits just want to visit loved ones to let them know they are fine, and they want the living to move and live their lives to the fullest."

"Marjorie, how do I pay you back for what you have done for my family? For what you have done for countless others?"

"All the money in the world could never match the satisfaction I receive when a surviving mother receives messages from her infant that died and who is now speaking from the afterlife to that mother. This alone is the real reason I speak to spirits. Everything else that transpires is only a bonus. Carlo, my heart is warmed by your wife seeking treatment because of the spirit's messages. I need no payment other than that."

"I know that, Marjorie. You are a rare breed in today's selfish, 'give me the world,' so I have a plan. My attorney, Gus Fauci, will take over for me if you allow him, please."

"Of course."

The attorney opens a folder and speaks.

"Marjorie, Carlo wants to do something special in recognition of what you have done for Angelina and him and all the others you help. So, Mr. DiLingo has come up with a plan that we feel you will love to be involved with."

Now I was getting really nervous. What could the main mafia man want with me? I don't want to be in business with him, I thought. Did he think he was going to team up with me in my psychic business?

Gus Fauci continued, "So we are proposing to you this. Mr. DiLingo would like to open a new grade school in the poorest country of Africa and put your name on it, the Marjorie Chapman School, in Malawi, Africa."

"I don't understand," I said, dumbfounded.

"Marjorie," Carlo said, "I will pay for a school to be built and run in Malawi, Africa, which is bordered by Zambia. This is the poorest country in Africa. These children there have nothing. We want them to have an education to better themselves. Will you let us put your name on the school? You will visit it once it has been built and regularly after it is up and running."

"That is so sweet of you, Carlo. You don't need my name on the school, but it is a nice gesture of you."

"You are an angel from heaven. You do so much good. It is an honor to have your name involved. Look at all the good we could do."

"But it must be very expensive?"

"Marjorie, there is a time in life when you feel you must give back," Carlo said. "I am a very wealthy man, I will admit. But if I die tonight, that money does nothing for me. I want these young children in grades one through nine to have a chance at a better life, careers, and the ability to move out of that poor country. God was good to my wife and me. I must do this. I will spend millions to get it done."

"Well, I agree. You can use my name if you wish. I would be proud and honored to have my name on a school like this."

"Now, can we eat? I'm starving!" Carlo laughed. "Every time I spend a fortune like this, I get famished."

"Yes," I agreed. "And when I see someone talking about spending a fortune, I get famished, too!" I joked.

We ate and chatted about Diaz and his total meltdown. Carlo promised he would have a contractor here in the morning to fix the bathroom and the door. I tried to tell him that he didn't have to fix anything.

"We like each other, right?" he asked.

"Yes, of course, Carlo."

"You don't want to hurt my feelings and offend me, do you?" He stood up with his six-foot-three frame.

"No way, my good man. I wouldn't think of offending you. Go ahead and fix it." I joked, knowing he was pulling my leg.

"Thank you, dear. It would be an honor to fix the damage and anything else my experts can improve upon.

"What else can I do for you, my love?" Carlo smiled as Gus looked, respectfully waiting for any and all requests I might have.

"Carlo, I need not a thing. I am a very happy woman, with so many loving friends, fans, and spirits that never let me rest."

"It must be so satisfying what you do. That is why I want to help hundreds of children get a better education. I need to give back to this world that has been so generous to me. I am an old man now, you know. I need to feel just a smattering of the satisfaction you feel. You know, Marjorie, you opened my eyes wide for the first time in a long time."

"Well, that warms my heart, Carlo. I do need to discuss some things with you."

"Of course, of course, anything, my dear."

"There are many spirit entities that are waiting patiently for their moment to communicate. Front and center and ready to burst is Virginia, the grandmother of Angelina. She is smiling and as excited as a child, Carlo. She is thrilled that you and Angelina have taken her message of a health scare so seriously."

"We owe her everything," Carlo said.

"Yes, we do. We are so fortunate that spirits stay with us, watch over us, and care so much. There is also someone front and center with Virginia. They are holding hands, Carlo. The spirit is calling out to you. He is a big man in stature, not only tall, but large. He goes by the name of Angelo. He has a thick full head of hair and says he was age 47 when he passed."

"That is my father. My God, Dad! Please tell him how much I love and miss him."

"He knows every thought you have. He tells me that he is with you for every tough decision that you ever make. He is proud of you."

"My father, Angelo, passed away at age 47 from a heart attack. It was very sudden and very devastating to our family. I loved my father very much. I looked up to him. I was only twenty when he died. I will admit it here, and now, I was very bitter and mad after my father died.

"I turned against God, friends, and even family. I blamed the whole world for losing my father. I turned to alcohol and was a bad drunk in those early days. Everyone, when I was twenty, had their father. How dare anyone take him from me? I was tough in those early days and used to get into knock-down, drag-out fights, barroom brawls every couple of days. Marjorie, I hated the world, and I joined the wrong gangs."

"Angelo knows this, and it hurt him greatly for those many years that, as he calls it, 'you were self-destructing.' But you did help yourself."

"It took many years before my hateful heart mellowed out considerably, though I did break many people's bones along the way. I did find peace, God, again, and a loving family that gave me something to live for.

"My father, Marjorie, was an extraordinary man. He worked two jobs, day and night, just to keep us fed, clothed, and sheltered. He was born in Palermo, Italy, and came here when he was 17 and unable to speak English. But he worked very hard and provided well for all of us. He had eight children, so it wasn't a party for him. I always wanted to be half the man he was. I never achieved the halfway mark, Marjorie. I'm still working on it. That is why we are doing the school in Africa."

"He admires your heroic change of attitude, as he puts it. He is pleased with your business. He says you built that window manufacturing business into an empire. No one could grow that business the way you did."

"It makes me very happy that my father has shown his approval. It means the world to me."

"Carlo, your father looks very sad right now. He is very worried about you."

"I don't understand."

"Yes, and Virginia is in agreement with him. They are telling me that you must walk away now."

"What do they want me to do? Walk away from my business?"

"Angelo is saying that you must retire from the dangerous business and slow down. He is saying that someone is looking to replace you as head of the family."

"So, they want me to step down as the head of the Litilio family? Someone is looking to kill me, yes?"

"They are showing me violent scenes, Carlo, of what might be planned by someone right now in their mind. Now I must warn you that spirit can see into the thoughts of so many individuals. This does not mean that the thoughts of some will actually be acted upon now, or possibly ever. Still, there are intentions out there. Angelo is saying that you have outlived your usefulness in the minds of many."

"I'm not scared of dying, Marjorie."

"Well, what they are showing me is quite gruesome, now. I see a body being cut into little pieces. I again caution, these are only thoughts in the minds of certain individuals. They may never come into play."

"Again, I am not scared of dying. I'm almost eighty in a couple of years. No one scares me anymore. I led a full life."

"Virginia and Angelo are showing me a picture of Angelina and you at a doctor's office. Angelina needs all the love and support you can shower upon her. Now and in the nerve-wracking future, extensive treatments ahead of her."

"Yes, I know that. I have been very concerned about being there for my wife."

"Angelo says you have been thinking about backing away from the crime family for years. He says it is time."

"I have been thinking about a great many things for years. I must admit, with the diagnosis of Angelina, I am very close to making the decision to step away. I may go full-time into the window company and our new school project. So, Dad, I hear you. I love you, and I want you to be proud of me."

I was happy that good things were happening. I felt somewhat responsible. I was sad about the Angel Diaz's loss of life. I felt responsible, though the spirits kept telling me that we cannot change everyone and every occurrence that was meant to be carried out.

But, overall, I was satisfied with my life, with my spirit guide Holly, who is my guiding strength. And I am proud of what I do, the outcomes of my readings for clients and their spirit entities., I am content with the life I have lived, the love I have projected to others over all the years.

And finally, when it is my time to go, I will be carried away by my family spirits and Holly, and I will know I gave all I could to society in "the end."

The End

CPSIA information can be obtained
at www.ICGtesting.com
Printed in the USA
BVHW041609231121
622346BV00017B/796